CAPTAIN BLOOD

Captain Blood

ISBN-13: 978-1944540937

For performance rights, contact drice@firstfolio.org
For more information, visit captainbloodplay.com

Published by Sordelet Ink
WWW.SORDELETINK.COM

CAPTAIN BLOOD

A PLAY BY
DAVID RICE

ADAPTED FROM THE NOVEL BY
Raphael Sabatini

SORDELET
ink

CAPTAIN BLOOD made its world premiere at First Folio Theatre, Oak Brook, Illinois, on January 28, 2017, directed by Janice L. Blixt. Scenic design was by Angela Weber Miller; original music and sound design was by Christopher Kriz; properties design was by Scott Leaton; costume design was by Alexa Weinzerle; the assistant stage manager was Anna Jones; lighting design was by Greg Freeman; fight direction was by Nick Sandys; and projection design was by Erin Pleake. The stage manager was Amy Creuziger, the assistant stage manager was Sarah West. The cast was as follows:

Dr Peter (Captain) Blood–Nick Sandys
Arabella Bishop–Heather Chrisler
Colonel Bishop–Aaron Christensen
Hagthorpe/Don Miguel–Kevin McKillip
Ogle–Jaq Seifort
Wolverstone–Christopher Jones
Jeremy Pitt–Austin England
Lord Julian–Sam Krey
Mary Trail / Dr. Whacker–Jennifer Mohr
Don Esteban–Christopher Vizurraga
Don Diego–Almanya Narula

Ensemble of Pirates, Spaniards, Frenchmen, Slaves, and Villains: Aaron Christensen, Kevin McKillip, Jaq Seifort, Christopher Jones, Austin England, Sam Krey, Jennifer Mohr, Christopher Vizurraga, Almanya Narula

FOR INFORMATION ABOUT PRODUCTION RIGHTS,
EMAIL DRICE@FIRSTFOLIO.ORG.

First Folio Theatre

Cast of Characters

Dr. Peter Blood: The hero! What more needs to be said?

Arabella Bishop: Mid-20's, which was old for an unmarried woman of her time. "She used with all men a sisterly frankness which in itself contains a quality of aloofness rendering it difficult for any man to become her lover."

Colonel Bishop: Sadistic plantation owner, Arabella's uncle

Governor Steed: Pleasant but ineffective governor of Port Royal, Jamaica

Hagthorpe (Narrator 1): Bumbling sailor

Pitt: Navigator; former Midshipman, so he's of the upper middle class, son of a successful merchant

Wolverston (Narrator 2): One-eyed giant

Ogle (Narrator 3): Gunner; has been around naval ships his entire life

Gardner (Slaver): Clever, but a bit of a whiner

Plummer (Overseer): Cruel and sadistic

Dr. Whacker: An officious, vainglorious man whose intelligence is even less than his detractors credit him for.

Don Diego de Panadero: Captain of the Cinco Llagas (The Five Wounds, referring to the five wounds of Christ). Aristocratic, scheming, a man not to be trusted

Esteban de Panadero: Young son of Don Diego

Don Alán de Panadero: Bother to Don Diego and Captain of the Encarnacion. Twin to his brother in every way

Lord Julian Willoughby: In his 30's or 40's; representative of the English Crown; an elegant but down-to-earth member of the ruling class; he carries himself with the easy assurance of a man of rank; a possible rival for Arabella's affections

Misc. Pirates, Sailors, and Citizens of the Town

SETTING

The set consists of multiple levels. The original production included sail-shaped surfaces which were used for the projection of visual elements. It also contained two raised areas on either side of the stage which were used, at times, to represent opposing ships. Between these side areas and the main playing deck were well padded pits representing the sea. These provided a handy place for bodies to ball or be rolled off the ship's deck, etc. allowing for ease of escape. The upstage area was highest and contained a short ship's rail and the ship's wheel, with exits L and R. This area (the poopdeck, as it were) was accessible by a single step on L and R of the main deck. Just at the USC area of the main deck was a series of step leading below the poopdeck, another easy place to roll out dead bodies and to provide entrance to ship's cabins, etc. The downstage area was a planked dock-like walkway leading to exits L and R. Action is continuous, with blackouts only at the end of each act.

ACT I

Scene One

(In the course of this opening, we meet the three main narra-tors. While each is a pirate, they must each have a distinct, specific character and voice, with separate and distinct accents. They are not simply generic "pirates." With the exception of Wolverston and the Spanish characters, I will not always write in dialect, to allow the actors to discover the characters' voices. However, none of them is American)

(The lights come up on a solitary sailor/pirate. He speaks with a working class English accent, perhaps of Portsmouth or Hampshire or elsewhere in south/southeast England. He is definitely not Cockney)

HAGTHORPE
Peter Blood, bachelor of medicine and several other things besides, smoked a pipe and tended the geraniums boxed on the sill of his window above Water Lane. In the narrow street below a stream of men gathered to join the ragtag group of rebels known as King Monmouth's Army. "Quo, quo, scelesti, ruitis" Blood murmured to himself as he watched....

(A second sailor/pirate enters the light and interrupts him. He might have a rough accent with tinges of Jamaica or somewhere else in the Caribbean)

WOLVERSTON
"Quo, quo" what?

HAGTHORPE
"Quo, quo, scelisti, ruitis." It's Latin. It means, "Oh where, oh where are you madmen rushing?"

WOLVERSTON
Y'ur not fixin' to start that way, are ya?

HAGTHORPE
It's the beginning of the story.

WOLVERSTON
Well, it's a bloody boring beginning, ain't it? I mean these folks seem nice 'n all, but they'll be a'bolting for the exit 'fore intermission if you do this.

HAGTHORPE
But they need the background, don't they?

WOLVERSTON
(To the audience) His name is Peter Blood, he's a doctor who used to be a soldier and they'll find out the rest as we tell the story. Got it? *(Back to HAGTHORPE)* You just don't start a pirate story like this.

HAGTHORPE
How do you start it? *(Hesitates)* I know!

(Spoken simultaneously)
HAGTHORPE
With a song!

WOLVERSTON
With a pirate battle!

(They argue for a brief instance. OGLE enters, clonks them both on the head. OGLE has an Irish accent, perhaps)

OGLE
You dolts! You don't start with a song OR a pirate battle.

They look at Ogle confused and then all say in unison.

ALL
You start with a song AND a pirate battle!

(The opening song about Captain Blood begins)

THE BALLAD OF CAPTAIN BLOOD

Come hear the tale of Captain Blood, a pirate bold
and brave.
He sailed the Caribbean Sea, a'tryin' to cheat the
grave.
If you should cross the man called Blood,
he'll chase you cross the swell
Rapaciously, tenaciously, and all the way to hell!

James Second was the sodding king in 1685,
And a more perfidious scoundrel on the throne did
ne'er survive.
James told his courts to sentence Blood to slave for
twenty year,
But Blood escaped and took to the sea and now
James quakes with fear.

CHORUS
For it's CAPTAIN BLOOD who's the pirate they
all dread.
He'll plunge in pursuit, then plunder your loot, and
leave your ship for dead
And it's BLOOD, BLOOD, BLOOD 'cross the sea
and 'neath the sky.

So it's Captain Blood we'll trust and love and follow
'til we die.

(Fight break)

From Barbados to Grenada he would sail in search
of plunder
And when bounty ships he spotted, how his cannons
they would thunder.
From the isle of Hispaniola all along the bounding
Main
To the Islands of the Virgin he harassed both France
and Spain.

The Spanish ship that we attacked contained a
golden hoard
So we sailed her down, and some we drowned, and
the rest put to the sword.
Then we pillaged all the booty, sank her in the deep
blue sea,
Now we're the boldest pirates in the world of infamy.

CHORUS
For it's CAPTAIN BLOOD who's the pirate they
all dread.
He'll plunge in pursuit, then plunder your loot, and
leave your ship for dead
And it's BLOOD, BLOOD, BLOOD 'cross the sea
and 'neath the sky.
So it's Captain Blood we'll trust and love and follow
'til we die.

(Fight break)

And it's BLOOD, BLOOD, BLOOD 'cross the sea
and 'neath the sky.
So it's Captain Blood we'll trust and love and follow

'til we die.

For it's BLOOD, BLOOD, BLOOD, yes it's BLOOD, BLOOD, BLOOD,
CAPTAIN BLOOD!

SCENE TWO

(From here on out, accents/voices should be chosen to fit each individual character, but all efforts must be made to avoid stereotypical, generic voices. Be specific)

(The end of the of the song/battle is the reveal of PETER BLOOD, who is seen with a scraggly beard, unkempt hair, ragged clothes, with manacles on his wrists, ready for the slave auction. Other men are also on display, all looking equally bedraggled. GARDNER, the slave auctioneer, is berating the men and beating them. GARDNER is fawning with his betters and cruel with his inferiors)

GARDNER
What are you ladies doing standing around? Come on, get in line! What are you gawking at? Get down there. Smile pretty for the customers. *(Comes to BLOOD)* Ah, it's you.

(Pushes BLOOD down to his knees)

GARDNER
Mind your manners, cur.

(GARDNER starts to walk away. BLOOD stands up)

GARDNER
I told you to mind your manners.

(He hits BLOOD and forces him down again. While all this is happening COLONEL BISHOP enters, as GARDNER, and ARABELLA BISHOP follows along behind him. BISHOP appears to be strong willed, but it is a façade to cover his own insecurities and fears. ARABELLA is feisty, confident, and full of life. She has an air of gentility about her, but it is tempered by having spent almost her entire life in the rough and tumble world of a Caribbean plantation)

GARDNER
Colonel Bishop! Surely there must be a few more of these fine specimens you can use for your sugar plantation, Colonel Bishop. It's the finest lot of prisoners I've had for sale in months.

BISHOP
And every one of them traitor to our good king, sentenced to ten years servitude for their crimes. The rest of these swine aren't fit for the labor on my plantation. No, I've bought the only strong ones you had for sale. Let Crabston have the rest.

ARABELLA
Crabston? Oh, uncle, not him. These men won't last a year under his lash.

BISHOP
These men are rebels against the king. They should be hanged, drawn, and quartered. Any other sentence is too good for them.

(ARABELLA stops in front of BLOOD and taps his arm with her riding crop)

ARABELLA
What about this one, Uncle?

BISHOP
Bah! A bag of bones. What should I do with him?

GARDNER
(Eager to make a sale) He's lean, but he's tough. When half of them was sick and the other half sickening on the trip over the sea, this rogue kept his legs and doctored his fellows. He's a real doctor, he is!

ARABELLA
He doesn't look like the kind of man the climate will kill, Uncle. And if he really is a doctor...

(GOVERNOR STEED has entered, unseen by all except BLOOD, who has watched him limping in, heavily dependent upon his cane)

GOVERNOR
(Chuckling) Trust your niece, Bishop! The fairer sex knows a real man when it sees one. And Lord knows we could use another doctor.

BISHOP
And why is that, when we've already got one in the town?

BLOOD
Because he's incompetent.

(BISHOP starts to raise his stick to strike BLOOD, but is cut off by the GOVERNOR. In all of this, BLOOD never flinches)

GOVERNOR
Hold off there, Bishop. *(To BLOOD)* What makes you say that?

BISHOP
Why even bother listening to this ragamuffin, as if a man who looks like that could know a thing or two about medicine.

BLOOD
Stultus est qui stratum, non equum inspicit.

BISHOP
Don't you go flinging your French at me!

(GOVERNOR laughs)

GOVERNOR
It's not French, Bishop, it's Latin. Seneca the Elder, I believe.

BLOOD
The younger, actually.

GOVERNOR
Ah yes. Let me see if I can translate it properly. "The man who inspects a saddle blanket instead of the horse is"...ummm...Stultis....stultis. Oh yes. Foolish. So I ask again, what makes you say my doctor is incompetent.

BLOOD
Because he's been treating your gout and you're still in pain.

GOVERNOR
How did you know I've got gout?

BLOOD
Because I'm a doctor. Let me guess, he started by using poultices of cow dung? And when those didn't work he switched to an ointment of wolworts and urine, I would wager? Let's see, after that he swore you'd be fine with a stocking full of nettles steeped in vinegars?

GOVERNOR
Precisely! Each one was worse than the previous ones...
and with the smell, my wife hasn't been able to stand
sleeping with me for weeks.

BLOOD
He's a quack. Were I your doctor, I could have your gout
relieved in two weeks. Alas, I'm not your doctor.

ARABELLA
See, Uncle. Buy this one, and then send him to treat
Governor Steed. I'm sure the governor will be grateful.

(The GOVERNOR smiles an acknowledgment. BISHOP
considers, then turns to GARDNER)

BISHOP
I'll give you five pounds for him.

GARDNER
Five pounds! He's worth twenty-five pounds if he's
worth a shilling!

BISHOP
Five pounds, or you can sell him to Crabston, who will
work him to death inside of a month.

GARDNER
Crabston will give me ten pounds for him.

BISHOP
Then let him.

(BISHOP starts to leave)

ARABELLA
Ten pounds it is.

GARDNER
I beg your pardon, Miss Arabella?

BISHOP
What are you doing, Arabella?

ARABELLA
You may manage the plantation, Uncle, but I own it. Or
will, when I turn twenty-five. And I'm buying this man
for my plantation.

BISHOP
(In ill humor) What's your name, dog?

BLOOD
Blood. Peter Blood.

GOVERNOR
(Laughs) Doctor Blood! Couldn't be more fitting, eh,
Bishop. Get him cleaned up and send him along to me
tomorrow. Help an old man hobble home, won't you
Miss Bishop. *(They exit)*

BISHOP
You had best remember your job, Blood, or I'll whip
your back until it matches your name.

(BISHOP strikes BLOOD with his stick)

BLOOD
Oh, I'll remember, my dear Colonel. I'll remember.

TRANSITION TO SCENE THREE

HAGTHORPE

And Dr. Peter Blood was as good as his word. You see, he was an unusual doctor for his time—he actually read the works of other noted doctors! He had learned from the Byzantine physician Alexander of Tralles that a tincture of crocus would relieve the pain of gout and from the Dutchman Herman Boerhaave that simply cutting back on red wine and red meat would work wonders at relieving the curse that had inflicted its pain on the good governor.

(There's a silence while WOLVERSTON and OGLE stare at him)

HAGTHORPE

I'm doing it again, ain't I? *(They nod. He begins to rush)* Sorry. And in doing so, he became the Governor's favorite physician.

WOLVERSTON

And di'nt that jest earn him the enmity of Dr. Whacker, Bridgetown's only other physician, a quack who had now lost the most lucrative and prestigious patient he had, so he did. *(Pronounces all four syllables of "pres-ti-*

gi-ous")

OGLE

Alas, the praise of the governor was the only thing saving him fully from the wrath of Colonel Bishop, for men like the colonel always resent those they know deep down are their betters. But for now, the Colonel had to temper his wrath, biding his time until Blood gave him the proper excuse...for the lash.

HAGTHORPE

For the nonce, Colonel Bishop had found that there was more profit to be made by letting him pursue his trade than by working him on the plantation.

Scene Three

(We find BLOOD, now cleaned up and looking healthy, strolling along the road on his way back from treating the governor. ARABELLA is coming from the other direction, on her way to town. BLOOD steps aside to let her pass by, giving her a small nod of deference with just a hint of insouciance in his smile. ARABELLA passes him by, then pauses and turns back)

ARABELLA
I think I know you, sir.

BLOOD
A lady should know her own property.

ARABELLA
My property?

BLOOD
Indeed. Let me present myself. I am called Peter Blood, and I am worth precisely ten pounds. I know it because that is the sum you paid for me. It is not every man has the same opportunities of ascertaining his real value.

(He laughs)

ARABELLA
My god! And you can laugh about it?

BLOOD
It is an achievement, but then, I have not fared as ill as I might. And 'tis you I have to thank for my comparatively easy and clean condition. I must never forget that I am your property.

ARABELLA
You sound as though you resent my buying you instead of letting you go to Crabston's plantation.

BLOOD
I have had no lack of experiences in my life; but being bought and sold was a new one, and I was hardly in the mood to love my purchaser. Would you be so kind as to explain why you chose to intervene in my fate? There were, after all, dozens of men waiting to be sold.

ARABELLA
You did not seem…quite like the others.

BLOOD
I am not.

ARABELLA
Oh! You have a rather good opinion of yourself.

BLOOD
On the contrary. The others are all honest rebels. I am not. And that makes all the difference. I was snoring in my bed while they were trying to free England from an unclean tyrant.

ARABELLA
Sir! I think you are talking treason.

BLOOD
If you only think so, I'll try to be clearer in the future.

ARABELLA
There are those here who would have you flogged if they heard you.

BLOOD
The governor would never allow it. For I also treat his lady's megrims. And that gives him even more peace than relieving his own gout.

ARABELLA
(Hiding a smile unsuccessfully) But if you are not a rebel, how come you here.

(Lights come up on WOLVERSTON and HAGTHORPE, [and OGLE?] as BLOOD continues to tell his story [or some other way of showing them observing the action while commenting on it]. In any case, the key is that we hear the narrators but fail to hear BLOOD's full tale)

WOLVERSTON
See! I told you as we'd get to the back story!

HAGTHORPE
Shhhh! You'll make the audience miss it all.

(Lights come back up on BLOOD and ARABELLA, but narrators are still seen)

BLOOD
And so I was sentenced to twenty years work on this island.

(The narrators look disappointed and exit as their light fades)

ARABELLA
For nothing more than obeying your Hippocratic oath

and treating injured men?

BLOOD
But those men were rebels and so, in the eyes of the judge I was aiding and abetting the rebels.

ARABELLA
My God! What an infamy!

BLOOD
Oh, it's a sweet country, England under King James. All things considered, I prefer being here on Barbados. Here at least one can believe in God.

ARABELLA
Is that so difficult elsewhere?

BLOOD
Men make it so.

ARABELLA
Well, then I congratulate you on this easing of your misfortunes. But I must be on to Bridgetown.

BLOOD
(As he watches her depart) "Stone walls do not a prison make, nor iron bars a cage." And you are, after all, his niece.

TRANSITION TO SCENE FOUR

OGLE
And so things would have remained between them had not fate intervened...as it always must or else we wouldn't have much of a story.

WOLVERSTON
We'll be a'skippin' ahead two weeks now. An English man-o-war has just docked in Bridgetown, coming in to refit and restock after a fierce battle with a Spanish pirate ship.

HAGTHORPE
The dock is lined with wounded English sailors, as well as a few ragged Spanish pirates who managed to survive the encounter.

Scene Four

(*Lights come up on BLOOD, who is treating the Spanish prisoner when COLONEL BISHOP approaches him. BLOOD is swabbing his wounds and the man flinches. He looks frightened*)

BLOOD
Tranquilo, mi amigo.

PRISONER
Por que hace eso?

BLOOD
Que?

PRISONER
Ayundando el enimgo?

BLOOD
Helping the enemy? I see no enemy. And it's what I do. Es lo que hago.

PRISONER
Te puedes meter en problemas.

BLOOD
Get in trouble? I've already learned that, my friend. Just call me stubborn. *(The sailor looks quizzical, so BLOOD translates)* Obstinado, amigo.

BISHOP
Blood! What are you doing there!

BLOOD
Tending to this man's wounds.

BISHOP
I can see that, fool! Just as I can see that this man is a Spanish pirate. Who gave you leave to tend to this man?

BLOOD
I am a doctor, Colonel Bishop. The man is wounded. It is not for me to discriminate. I keep to my trade.

BISHOP
Do you, by God! If you'd done that, you wouldn't now be here!

BLOOD
On the contrary, Colonel. It's precisely because I tended to the wounds of men who turned out to be rebels that I was sentenced to your…kindness.

BISHOP
Aye, I know your lying tale. You claim not to have been a rebel yourself. As if that matters. Cease that and look at me when I'm speaking.

(BLOOD continues to minister to the prisoner, never looking at BISHOP)

BLOOD
This man is in pain and I've been ordered to attend to all the men. *(In Spanish)* Tranquilo amigo, no hay que temer.

BISHOP
And I'm ordering you to stop!

(*BISHOP raises his cane to strike BLOOD, but the GOVERNOR has entered behind him*)

GOVERNOR
I fear, Colonel Bishop, that in this instance, my orders outweigh yours. And there's no more to be said.

BISHOP
There's a great deal more to be said, sir! What do you mean allowing this so-called doctor to give comfort and aid to the enemy. He doesn't deserve care, he deserves to be thrown back out to sea and drowned.

GOVERNOR
You talk like a Spaniard, Colonel, not an Englishman.

(*And this insult is so great that BISHOP is rendered speechless and exits*)

GOVERNOR
Carry on, Dr. Blood.

(*As this has been happening, we see ARABELLA giving water to the other men, using a gourd of water. As THE GOVERNOR exits, she crosses to BLOOD's patient and begins to help the man drink*)

BLOOD
I think you're mistaken, Miss Bishop. This man's a Spaniard.

ARABELLA
So I perceive. But he's a human being none the less.

BLOOD
Your uncle is of a different mind. He regards them as vermin to be left to languish and die of their festering

wounds.

ARABELLA
And you thought, of course, that I must be of my uncle's mind?

BLOOD
I'd not willingly be rude to a lady, even in my thoughts. But I thought you might want to consider the consequences should your uncle hear of it.

ARABELLA
First you impute to me inhumanity and then cowardice. For a man who would not "willingly be rude to a lady," you're doing a pretty poor job of complimenting me.

BLOOD
Then let me try this. How was I to guess that Colonel Bishop would have an angel for a niece?

ARABELLA
From everything I see, I shouldn't think you often guess aright. You must be careful, or your guesses will take you to your grave. *(Exits)*

PRISONER
Ella es bonita, Doctor, pere es fogosa.

BLOOD
(Repeats Spanish word for "beautiful and fiery" quizzically) Bonita y fogosa? No, amigo. Not beautiful and fiery. She is beautiful because she is fiery!

(The wounded PRISONER is helped off. As BLOOD turns to leave, he is hailed by DR. WHACKER. WHACKER is a sycophantic man, just this side of being a fop)

WHACKER
Ho, good doctor!

BLOOD
Do you call to me, good Dr. Whacker?

(BLOOD gives a highly formal bow to WHACKER)

WHACKER
Indeed, sir, I do. I have been seeking for you, to ask some advice, as one sagacious medical brother to another. And perhaps to offer some, as well.

BLOOD
You'll forgive me, sir, if I seem a bit taken aback. I was under the apprehension that you were, shall we say, out of sorts with me for poaching our good governor and his wife.

WHACKER
Ah, that sir. Well, I have to say I am not surprised by that latter, sir. Youth and good looks, Doctor Blood! Youth and good looks! They are inestimable advantages in our profession as in others—especially where the ladies are concerned.

BLOOD
If you mean what you seem to mean, you had better say it to Governor Steed.

WHACKER
You misapprehend me! I desire to be your friend. This slavery in which you find yourself is…irksome. I have seen it in your eyes, sir.

BLOOD
How perceptive, sir, to be able to tell that a slave resents his servitude.

WHACKER
It's a gift, sir. How often have I seen you staring out at the sea. I know what on what you are ruminating, sir, oh

indeed I do, sir. Indeed, I do. The world is a capacious place. There are many nations besides England where a man of your aptitude would be warmly welcomed. For example, it is none so far now to the Dutch settlement of Curacao. At this time of year the excursion may be safely undertaken in a light craft.

BLOOD
And where, pray tell, would a man such as I find such a craft?

WHACKER
Did I not say that I desired to be your friend as well as your colleague?

BLOOD
Indeed, you did, sir. As one fellow follower of Galen to another, as it were. And the loss of business is as of nothing to you, I am sure.

WHACKER
Precisely, sir! You apprehend my motives indeed. So if a craft were made available, say, next week…? You agree, sir, that this might be fortuitous?

BLOOD
If I should be caught and brought back, they'd clip my wings and brand me for life.

WHACKER
Surely, sir, the reward of the enterprise is worth a little risk?

BLOOD
Surely. But it asks more than courage. It asks money. Now if I were to have access not only to a small craft, but to a small sum of money…

WHACKER
Say fifteen pounds, sir?

BLOOD
Oh sir, I think a sum of some thirty pounds might better serve my needs.

WHACKER
(Clearly nonplussed) Thirty pounds sir? That would be my whole savings, sir!

BLOOD
But for the safety and freedom of a fellow practitioner of the arts of Hippocrates and Galen? For a fellow descendant of the Greek god Aesclepius?

WHACKER
(Sighing) Done, sir. Done. Such a craft, well provisioned, shall be awaiting you in the cove, sir. But I can only risk leaving it there for one night, sir. Any longer and it would be found by the authorities and confiscated. So your escape, nay, let us say your departure, shall we? Your departure must be exactly one week from tonight, sir. And may God be rid of you. I mean, may God be *with* you.

BLOOD
And God's blessings be with your patients...sir. *(BLOOD starts to leave and then turns back)* One more thing, good Doctor. A simple-minded soul might think this a good chance to use trickery to have me arrested. But an intelligent and learned man would remember in what esteem the governor holds me...and how much my word would mean against his. Heigh ho for the governor's foot! *(Claps WHACKER on the back)* Good day, sir! *(Exits)*

TRANSITION TO SCENE FIVE

WOLVERSTON
Now little did that greedy bugger Whacker know that Peter would've taken him up on his offer without so much as a single piece of eight.

HAGTHORPE
Because Peter had been conspiring for weeks with a number of his fellow slaves to escape.

OGLE
Indeed, he had assembled an entire crew, all of them more than willing to risk their beleaguered lives in order to escape the floggings regularly visited on them by Colonel Bishop.

HAGTHORPE
His crew included more than a few men who had formerly been members of the King's own Royal Navy before being declared rebels. *(Each man is revealed in light as introduced? Some of the men are the narrators?)* There was, me, Josiah Hagthorpe, an able seaman and a man who knows the ways of the mast and the rigging.

OGLE
And me, gunner's mate Ogle, with the deadliest eye in

the Caribbean.

WOLVERSTON
And he was thankin' the lord as he'd included me, the one-eyed giant Wolverston!

OGLE
But most importantly, the crew included Jeremy Pitt, the young navigator and former midshipman.

HAGTHORPE
For in the endless oceans, once out of sight of land, a ship was lost without its navigator.

WOLVERSTON
For by god, without a navigator, there was none of them plans as stood a chance.

OGLE
Alas, the only man on the planation that Colonel Bishop reviled as much as Peter Blood was the youth, Jeremy Pitt, because the sight of men of honor will always make men like Colonel Bishop see themselves as they really are.

Scene Five

(COLONEL BISHOP, carrying a whip, and his overseer come across JEREMY PITT cutting sugar cane with a machete)

BISHOP
(Addressing PITT) You there, Pitt. Where the devil is Blood.

PITT
I'm sure I don't know, Colonel.

BISHOP
Bollocks! You two are always thick as thieves. What is Blood up to and where is he?

PITT
I'll have to plead Genesis 4, verse 9, Colonel.

BISHOP
What are you talking about, you insolent cur? What's the Bible got to do with answering my question?

PITT
Then the Lord said to Cain, "Where is your brother Abel?" "I don't know," he replied. "Am I my brother's keeper?"

BISHOP
Impudent dog. Trifle with me, will you? D'you think I'm to be mocked? I'll teach you a lesson.

(BISHOP raises his whip to thwack PITT, and PITT instinctively raises his arm to ward off the blow. However, the arm he raises is the one holding the machete he was using to cut cane)

BISHOP
Threaten me with that machete, will you? Plummer, tie him up. A mutinous cur that shows his fangs to his master must learn good manners at the cost of a striped hide. Plummer tie him up. You'll be a good example for the others, Pitt.

(PITT looks around as if to run, but realizes he has no choice but to obey. He is led upstage where the overseer lashes his hands to [what will be] the ship's rail)

BISHOP
Now we'll see if we can release some of that insolence from you.

(BISHOP begins to lash PITT as the lights fade on this scene)

SCENE SIX

(The scene changes to focus on BLOOD coming along the road back to the plantation with ARABELLA coming towards him heading into town. He stops to speak to her, knowing that this may be the last time they speak)

BLOOD
Good morrow, Miss Arabella.

ARABELLA
Ah, so it's Miss Arabella, now, is it? What happened to Miss Bishop?

BLOOD
Miss Bishop? She floated away, popped like a bubble by the intrusion of reality.

ARABELLA
You make too free, Dr. Blood.

BLOOD
A doctor's prerogative.

ARABELLA
Your attitude has changed, it seems, since we last met,

when was it?

BLOOD
Exactly one week ago.

ARABELLA
I hadn't realized it had been that long. My mind was on other things.

BLOOD
Such as?

ARABELLA
Trying to ascertain why you speak such excellent Spanish, for one.

BLOOD
Is that all? I was two years in a Spanish jail.

ARABELLA
In jail?

BLOOD
As a prisoner of war. I was in the French service at the time.

ARABELLA
But you're a doctor!

BLOOD
That's merely a diversion, I think. By trade, I am a soldier, and for a time I found some freedom to pursue that occupation with the French navy. For that seems to be the life I'm fit for and it's served me no worse than medicine, for both brought me into prison. And from all I've seen, it appears that it must be more pleasing in the sight of Heaven to kill men than to heal them.

(They are interrupted by HAGTHORPE)

HAGTHORPE
Peter, come quick! *(He spies ARABELLA)* Oh, beg your
pardon, Miss Bishop, as I didn't see you standing there.

BLOOD
What is it, Hagthorpe. What's wrong? *(HAGTHORPE
is clearly hesitant)* Out with it man, what's the matter?

HAGTHORPE
It's Pitt. He's run afoul of that bast…of the Colonel.
The Colonel just gave him fifty lashes and now he's tied
to a post in the yard. As a warning to the rest of us, the
Colonel says. And he's to stay tied up there for two days.

*(BLOOD begins to laugh, filled with the knowledge that
without PITT, their plans are useless)*

ARABELLA
And why do you laugh, sir?

BLOOD
A man must sometimes laugh at himself or go mad. Few realize it. That is why there are so many madmen in the world.

ARABELLA
I feared you were laughing at me.

BLOOD
I laugh only at the comic, Miss Arabella, and you are
not comical.

ARABELLA
What am I, then?

BLOOD
You are the lady who owns me. And you'd best be off to
town, m'lady, and not be caught lollygagging here with
your poor servant. *(He then takes her hand and kisses it,
turns, and exits without another word)*

Scene Seven

(Lights fade back up on PITT, who is still tied up the rail, his shirt is torn and bloody indicating the wounds to his back. We hear the sound of flies buzzing around. BLOOD and HAGTHORPE run in. HAGTHORPE has a knife and BLOOD carries a gourd bottle of water. They cut PITT down and slowly lower him to the ground, until PITT and BLOOD are seated side by side with PITT's head on BLOOD's shoulder)

PITT
Drink! Oh god, give me drink, for the love of Christ. (Tries to sit up to drink, but this causes the pain in his back to flare up. He writhes in agony) My back! Christ on the cross, my back!

BLOOD
Be easy, Jeremy. We'll take care of your back in a moment. But first, take some of this water.

PITT
"Blessed are the merciful, for they shall obtain mercy." Matthew 5.

BLOOD
Oh, lad. Why did you provoke that man.

PITT
I'm sorry, Peter. But he's had it in for me since you and I came here. I'm afraid you'll have to go without me tonight.

BLOOD
You think we can make it without our navigator, Jeremy? And even if we could, do you think I'd abandon you? Bad cess to that filthy slaver! We'll find a way, Jeremy, I promise you.

(COLONEL BISHOP enters and sees BLOOD and PITT)

BISHOP
What the devil are you doing here?

BLOOD
Doing? Why, the duties of my office. *(He continues to give PITT water)*

BISHOP
I said he was to have neither meat nor drink until I ordered it.

BLOOD
Surely, sir, I never heard you. All that I knew was that one of your slaves was being murdered by the sun and the flies. And I said to myself, "This is one of the Colonel's slaves; I'm the Colonel's doctor; it's my duty to be looking after the Colonel's property." I assume that's right, Colonel?

BISHOP
Right?!

BLOOD
Be easy now, Colonel, or you'll give yourself an attack
of apoplexy with those splenetic and bilious outbursts,
and then I'll have two patients to minister to.

BISHOP
By God! Do you dare take that tone with me, you dog?
I've been too soft with you. It's time you tasted the lash
yourself. I'll flog you until there's not an inch of skin
left...

(BISHOP's outburst is interrupted by the sound of cannon
fire. Both men stop and look around, finally catching sight
of a ship in the town's harbor which is firing its cannons
on the town. PLUMMER comes running)

PLUMMER
Colonel! Spanish pirates are in the harbor attacking
Bridgetown!

BISHOP
Are you mad? How could they get that close?

PLUMMER
Sailed in under false colors. Once their crew was ashore,
the ship opened fire on the barracks. Most of the garri-
son was caught there. The town is ablaze. Half those
Spanish Papists are attacking the governor's mansion
while the rest of them are terrorizing the town!

BISHOP
Gather the rest of my men and meet me at the harbor!

(BISHOP and PLUMMER exit. BLOOD gestures
HAGTHORPE over and they help Pitt to his feet)

BLOOD
Take Pitt with you. Get him and the rest of the men to
our boat. I'll meet you there.

HAGTHORPE
Where are you going?

BLOOD
Into town.

HAGTHORPE
For God's sake, why?

BLOOD
I think someone might need my help.

Scene Eight

(The streets of Bridgetown, where the Spanish are busy sacking the town. We see a trio of Spanish buccaneers racing through town chasing a young woman. They trap her in a corner and begin making their intentions clear with rude remarks)

SPANIARD 1
(Chuckling lewdly) Ven señorita, no te queremos hacer daño.

SPANIARD 2
Somos marineros que no han tenido compania en mucho tiempo.

(BLOOD sneaks up behind one of them)

BLOOD
Soy doctora señor, and I can cure that love ache of yours.

(And when the man turns, BLOOD kicks him in the crotch, grabs his sword out of his hand, and stabs him. The other two men turn to challenge BLOOD. There is a short fight where BLOOD manages to hold his own for a

moment, but the two refuse to be fully baited and eventually work their way around so that there is one on either side, leaving BLOOD in a conundrum)

BLOOD
(Now speaking English?) Well, my Spanish amigos. I don't suppose you'd consider making this a fair fight and taking me on one at a time.

SPANIARD 1
Perro Ingles! You are not as amusing as you think you are.

BLOOD
So I've been told, my friend, so I've been told.

(Just as the Spaniards start to close in on BLOOD, ARABELLA enters, with her hands behind her back)

ARABELLA
Perdoname, Señores. Could you help direct me to a place of safety?

SPANIARD 2
I promise you, Señorita, you'll have all the protection you will ever need after we take care of the English dog.

SPANIARD 1
And perhaps you'll have a reward for us?

ARABELLA
I've got the perfect reward for a man like you, sir.

(She reveals the sword that she has been keeping hidden behind her back and immediately engages the Spaniard closest to her, while BLOOD engages the other. After a few passes, ARABELLA and BLOOD end up back to back both manage to throw off their attackers far enough/in a way which gives them a momentary breather. They hold this conversation while continuing to fend off the Spaniards. The

actual fight should be a few moves followed by the Spaniards regrouping while BLOOD and ARABELLA say a few lines, then another sequence, etc)

BLOOD
You are full of surprises!

ARABELLA
A woman has to keep a few secrets. How else will she keep a man confused?

BLOOD
Don't tell me the Colonel taught you this?

ARABELLA
(Laughing) My uncle? Not on your life. My father. It was a game he liked to play, said it might come in handy someday.

BLOOD
And what, pray tell, happened to him?

ARABELLA
Fever, when I was twelve. And that's when he sent for my uncle, to run the plantation until I reached my majority at the age of twenty-five and could take over for myself.

BLOOD
And how long will that be?

ARABELLA
A lady never tells her age.

BLOOD
And this will teach you not to pick on a lady. *(BLOOD skewers his opponent)*

ARABELLA
Au contraire, Peter. *This* is how you teach someone not to pick on a lady. *(ARABELLA skewers her opponent)*

BLOOD
I stand corrected, my lady. Now take... *(He looks at the woman they have just rescued)*

LADY
Mary Trail, if you please.

BLOOD
Now take Mary-Trail-If-You-Please and make your way back to the plantation.

ARABELLA
Where are you going?

BLOOD
To keep an appointment.

(And again, he kisses her hand and departs. Leaving ARABELLA to lead a swooning MARY away)

ARABELLA
(Frustrated) Come along, Mary Trail. If you please!

TRANSITION TO SCENE NINE

HAGTHORPE
And while Peter was taking it easy onshore, I was busy gathering the men and leading them on a mission to capture the Spanish ship. There were thirty men on board, but they didn't stand a chance against Hagthorpe!

WOLVERSTON
Clears his throat.

HAGTHORPE
Okay, okay. You can't blame a fellow for trying. I mean, gobs of story tellers exaggerate for effect *(pronounces it "ee-fect")*. Look at that Shakespeare fellow.

OGLE
What he meant to say was that once the men had gathered, Peter led us down to the boat Whacker had left for us and silently rowed out to the Cinco Llagas *(pronounced CHIN-co YA-gas)* where there was naught but a skeleton crew left on board.

Scene Nine

(BLOOD climbs up the ladder into the opening in the rail and peeks over, seeing a solitary Spanish soldier who is drinking from a bottle. He climbs aboard and is about sneak up on the soldier when WOLVERSTON climbs up beside him, taps him on the shoulder, and indicates that he's got this one. WOLVERSTON sneaks up on the man, taps him on the shoulder. The soldier turns and is so scared he is speechless. Wolverston simply taps him on the head with a belaying pin and knocks him out. BLOOD, HAGTHORPE, and OGLE follow behind WOLVERSTON, they jump down and in the darkness we hear the sounds of a scuffle. When they come back up, they are wearing the caps of the Spanish sailors. BLOOD looks over the other side of the ship)

BLOOD
And none too soon, lads. Here comes the Spanish captain back with the first of his boats, and the rest not far behind! Ogle, get the rest of the crew onboard and man those guns and be quick about it! When I give you the word, blast the Spanish longboats out of the water. And

you'd better be as good as you say you are, Ogle.

OGLE
(Grinning) When I'm sober, Peter, there's none better.

BLOOD
The question is, are you sober?

OGLE
As sober as a priest. *(He exits)*

BLOOD
You look worried, Hagthorpe.

HAGTHORPE
I am sir. I've never known a sober Irish priest.

BLOOD
Get ready to welcome our guests.

(From below the rail we hear the voice of DON DIEGO, along with the sound of the longboat coming alongside the Cinco Llagas, and the men who are with DON DIEGO having a good time)

DON DIEGO:
¡Oye! ¡Bajar una cuerda y arrastrar el rescate!

BLOOD
Sí, capitán. ¡A tus órdenes!

(DON DIEGO comes on board. He hands up a chest of gold and then is helped aboard by BLOOD who pushes him over towards WOLVERSTON who hits him on the head)

BLOOD
Take the good captain to his cabin, Wolverston. Hagthorpe, hoist the English ensign. *(Shouting)* Ogle! FIRE!!

(We hear the sounds of cannon firing and men cheering as the lights fade. The fighting sounds continue for a moment then fade as the lights come up on the narrators)

TRANSITION TO SCENE TEN

WOLVERSTON
And wouldn't you know that squirt Ogle was as good as his word, and didn't he a'sink six of them eight Spanish longboats. The other two as managed to make it back to shore were forced to surrender to the Governor's men.

OGLE
Which left the Governor and the other people of Bridgetown to ask one another who had taken over the Spanish ship?

HAGTHORPE
And to answer this question, and convey their gratitude, they sent over a delegation to the Cinco Llagas led by...

Scene Ten

(Lights come up and we see COLONEL BISHOP being helped aboard. BLOOD is now dressed up in the elegant clothes he has taken from the cabin of DON DIEGO. He is standing with his back to BISHOP. As such, BISHOP does not recognize him until he starts to speak)

BISHOP
Greetings, sir. *(He bows)* I bring you the welcome and gratitude of the governor and all the good people of Bridgetown.

(BLOOD turns)

BLOOD
Welcome aboard the Cinco Llagas, my dear Colonel. We scarcely thought we would be lucky enough to have you as our guest. You find yourself among friends—old friends of yours all.

BISHOP
Blood! Then it was you...

BLOOD
It was, indeed, Colonel.

BISHOP
Oddswounds, this is heroic!

HAGTHORPE
Heroic? By God it's epic!

BISHOP
(*Spotting a chest on deck*) And you've not only captured the ship, you've recovered the ransom these pirates took from the town! God's my life, you deserve well for this and you'll not find us ungrateful.

BLOOD
Indeed. And how grateful shall we find you?

BISHOP
Why—I'm sure the governor will write to King James and ask him to remit some portion of your sentences.

HAGTHORPE
Ohhhh! The generosity of King James is well known!

(*All the men all laugh*)

OGLE
Come now, Hagthorpe. The Colonel has a kind heart. What kind we wouldn't want to say.

BLOOD
And there's another matter, that of the flogging that's due me. You're a man of your word in such matters, Colonel—if not perhaps in others—and you said, if I remember, that you'd not leave a square inch of skin on my back.

BISHOP
Tut, tut. After this splendid deed of yours, why speak

of that now?

BLOOD
Tut, tut, indeed, Colonel. Now would be the only time to talk of it. You've worked a good deal of cruelty in your time. Poor Jeremy Pitt was brought aboard with a back that's been flayed and he'll not be himself for days. And if not for the Spanish, he may have been dead by now...and maybe myself with him.

HAGTHORPE
Why waste words on this hog, Peter? Fling him overboard and have done with him.

WOLVERSTON
String him up from the yardarm! *(Others begin to yell in agreement)*

HAGTHORPE
Let the bilge rat dance a hempen jig!

OGLE
Just keelhaul the scoundrel!

WOLVERSTON
Aye! Let him give Neptune a salute!

BLOOD
The men appear to be in agreement with Prudentius, Colonel. "Vivere commune est, sed non commune mereri."

BISHOP
I told you, I don't speak French.

BLOOD
It's still Latin, Colonel. "Every man lives; not every man deserves to."

BISHOP
You wouldn't dare!

BLOOD
Oh, Colonel, sir, I certainly would dare!

(The men cheer and make to hang BISHOP)

BLOOD
Hold on men! If you please, Wolverston. While we were waiting for the Colonel, you all elected me captain. And as Captain, I'll conduct affairs in my own way. That's the pact, and I'll please you to all remember it. Or you can send me ashore, if you'd rather.

(The men respond in the negative)

BLOOD
Alright, then. I need the Colonel to stay alive and be my messenger.

BISHOP
I'll be damned if I will, Blood.

BLOOD
That's *Captain* Blood, sir. You may not have noticed, Colonel, but we slipped anchor as soon as you were on board and we're now well under way. We're about to pass out of the harbor, but we're close enough to the headland that you'll be able to swim ashore. You can swim, I hope, Colonel. When you get ashore, thank the Governor for his kindness. Oh, and please to convey this to your niece. *(He shoves a small pouch inside BISHOP's jacket)*

BISHOP
And what is this?

BLOOD
Ten pounds. Tell her I've bought myself back. Now, as your doctor, I prescribe a swim to cool the excessive heat of your humors.

(The men push/throw BISHOP overboard to great laughter and cheers)

HAGTHORPE
Cheers for Captain Blood! *(The men join in)* Hip hip, HOORAY!

(And they all begin to chant BLOOD! BLOOD! BLOOD! And the lights fade out and we have transition music which then fades out as the lights come up on our narrators)

TRANSITION TO SCENE ELEVEN

WOLVERSTON
But afore ye spit in the bucket, ye should know that as we sailed away from Barbados, Captain Blood was all too aware that we were all still a'making our escape to the Dutch island of Curacao.

OGLE
For the Cap'n knew that once we'd cleared Barbados and sailed through the archipelago, we'd be out of sight of land. And not a one of us had the skills to pilot our ship on its course.

HAGTHORPE
Fer poor Jeremy Pitt, our sole navigator, was still suffering from the flogging.

OGLE
Which is explainin' why Blood had set ashore all but two of the Spanish sailors.

HAGTHORPE
Don Diego the captain.

WOLVERSTON
And one other fancy pants officer, whose identity had

been pointed out to Blood by a member of the Spanish crew...after a little bit of persuadin'.

Scene Eleven

(Lights come up on BLOOD and DON DIEGO on the deck of the Cinco Llagas)

DIEGO
So now that you've set my men ashore, what are your plans? I think maybe they are not pleasant for me.

BLOOD
You are not afraid to die?

DIEGO
The question she offends, sir!

BLOOD
Then let me put it another way—do you not desire to live?

DIEGO
Ah, that I can answer. I do desire to live, but that desire shall not make a coward of me for your amusement.

BLOOD
And what about your son, Don Diego? Do you desire

him to live, as well?

DIEGO
My son?

BLOOD
Si, Señor, for I fear that you were not the only Spaniard kept aboard ship. Would you be willing to earn life and liberty not just for yourself, but for your son?

DIEGO
To earn it, do you say? If the service you propose does not hurt my honor...

BLOOD
Could I be guilty of that, sir? I realize that even a pirate has his honor.

DIEGO
I am not a pirate, sir! I am a Captain in the Royal Navy of His Catholic Majesty Carlos, King of Spain!

BLOOD
A man who acts like a pirate is a pirate, no matter what throne sanctions his behavior. But be that as you will. If you look out there, Don Diego, you will see what appears to be a small cloud on the horizon. That is the island of Saint Vincent, falling fast astern. And from here to Curacao there is no more land. The only man amongst us schooled in the art of navigation is fevered and delirious. I can handle a ship in action, but I never mastered the mysteries of the sextant and the art of finding a way over the trackless wastes of ocean.

DIEGO
So?

BLOOD
If you pledge me your honor to act as our navigator and

guide us to Curacao, I'll give you parole and let you have the run of the ship. And I give you my word I will release you and your son when we arrive there.

DIEGO
I accept.

TRANSITION TO SCENE TWELVE

HAGTHORPE
Over the next days, Don Diego proved to be both agreeable and proficient.

WOLVERSTON
At meals, that little popinjay even proved to be amusing.

OGLE
And so Blood was lulled into a sense of security.

HAGTHORPE
Still, all may have gone well had not the ship found itself caught in a storm.

(We now see and hear the storm and hear the men fighting to keep the ship safe. Video screen used here. The following dialogue should be pre-recorded heard over/during the storm, but without our actually seeing the men. Video projection/action choreographed like a dance)

BLOOD
All hands on deck! *(A crew member repeats the order, relaying it on)* Batten down those hatches! *(A different crew member repeats)*

WOLVERSTON
Mind that topgallant!

OGLE
Dog down those guns, men. One loose cannon rolling below decks'll be the death of us all

WOLVERSTON
Furl those sails faster, you pox-ridden knaves! Closehaul that jib, you bastards! Do I need to tell you twice.

DIEGO
It's getting hard to hold her steady, Captain.

BLOOD
You've got this, Don Diego. Keep her running. Hagthorpe, lend a hand for'ard!

HAGTHORPE
Aye, aye, Cap'n

BLOOD
Shorten the sail, Wolf! *(Crew member relays the order)*

WOLVERSTON
Take in the topgallants! Reef those nippersails, I said!

BLOOD
Tacks and braces, men! *(Crew member relays the order)* We need to run before the wind!!

(Storm sound/images grow during narration the narration and then begin to abate. The narration begins as the sounds of the storm subside)

WOLVERSTON
And when that pox-ridden wind had abated, all the Cap'n knew was as we had been blown badly off course.

OGLE
But Don Diego, ever a man of his word, assured Blood

that he knew where they needed to go.

HAGTHORPE
And so we sailed on and all seemed well.

WOLVERSTON
And good Jeremy Pitt even recovered to the point as he was able to come out'n his cabin one evenin' and join the Cap'n on deck.

(Light comes up to find the two of them on deck, PITT leaning on BLOOD's arm until he can sit down)

Scene Twelve

PITT
It's good to be up again, Peter.

BLOOD
And it's good to see you getting well, Jeremy. For a while there, we didn't think you'd make it! And if you hadn't, I would have been regretting letting the Colonel go after all.

PITT
You're a good man, Peter. Perhaps too good.

BLOOD
(Laughing) There are many as would argue with you there, Jeremy!

(As there have been talking, PITT has been looking at the sky and growing puzzled)

PITT
"He alone stretches out the heavens and treads on the waves of the sea. He is the Maker of the Bear and Orion, the Pleiades and the constellations of the

south." Job, Chapter 9. Do you know anything of astronomy, Peter?

BLOOD
Faith, I couldn't tell the Belt of Orion from the Girdle of Venus. Why do you ask?

PITT
(Pointing to spot over the starboard bow) That's the North Star.

BLOOD
Is it now? I wonder that you can pick it out from the thousands of others.

PITT
And with the North Star over our starboard bow, that means we're steering a course north northwest, or maybe north by west, for I doubt if we're standing more than 10 degrees westward.

BLOOD
(Pausing for a moment and stiffening) But shouldn't Curacao be to the southwest not the northwest?

PITT
Yes, Peter, it should.

(And just at that moment, DON DIEGO appears on deck. BLOOD puts a warning hand on PITT's shoulder)

BLOOD
Don Diego! You've arrived just in time. Could you settle a slight dispute between myself and Mr. Pitt.

DIEGO
I would be delighted to, if I am able. It is the least I can do to repay you for your hospitality.

BLOOD
We were just arguing, Mr. Pitt and I, as to which is the North Star.

DIEGO
But you tell me that Mr. Pitt is your Navigant, no? Should he not know?

PITT
I fear my recovery is not yet complete, sir, and my wits may still be addled. Would you be so kind as to point it out?

DIEGO
(Without hesitation or guile he points immediately to the correct spot) That is the star of the North, just off our starboard bow.

PITT
In that case, Don Diego, will you tell me why, if Curacao is our destination, we appear to be on this course?

DIEGO
You have reason to ask and I had hope' it would not be observe'. I have been careless after the storm. When I correct our course, I correct it too far and my error, I do not catch until this afternoon, and so we come by a half degree too far south. Had I not caught my error, we might have end up in Caracas! My negligence, I did not want to admit, but I fear you have caught me out. Now Curacao, she is almost due north. That is what has cause' the delay. We will be at our destination tomorrow, I assure you.

BLOOD
It's a fine man who can admit his error, Don Diego! Now let us all go below and toast to the end of our journey.

SCENE THIRTEEN

(Lights fade and there is a transition which ends with the sound of 4 ship's bells—2, pause, 2—which is 6:00 in the morning watch. We see CAPTAIN BLOOD and DON DIEGO come out and look over the bow on a sunny morning)

DIEGO
And there you are, Don Pedro. There is the Promised Land, as I...promised.

BLOOD
(Hearing something in DON DIEGO's voice) You find an odd satisfaction in the sight of it, all things considered.

DIEGO
Merely the satisfaction of a mariner.

(HAGTHORPE yells from offstage)

HAGTHORPE
Captain! The lookout says there's a ship coming up on us and it's flying the Spanish flag!

BLOOD
Ah. Rather, Don Diego, the satisfaction of a traitor. What land is that ahead?

DIEGO
The island of Hispaniola sir. And unless I miss my guess, the ship coming swiftly upon us is the Encarnacion, under the command of my brother Don Alán de Panadero, the Lord Admiral of Castille. The Almighty, you see, watches over the destinies of Catholic Spain.

BLOOD
Well, perhaps he'll also have a moment or two to look after a Protestant sinner as well.

(And with that he springs on BLOOD and the two have a "found object" fight. The original included fists, a harpoon, a piece of net, and a large rope with a big knot on the end. The fight ends with BLOOD besting his opponent just as HAGTHORPE and Wolverston arrive, having heard the scuffle)

BLOOD
Hagthorpe! Bring me Don Diego's son.

DIEGO
You underestimated me, Captain. (He says this last word mockingly) I tell you that I was not fear death, and I meant it, Perro Ingles!

BLOOD
And your word?

DIEGO
It means nothing given to a man such as you. Go ahead and kill me, if you wish.

(This is said just as DON ESTEBAN is brought on board by HAGTHORPE and OGLE)

ESTEBAN
No, Padre mio, no!

BLOOD
It seems your son may feel differently about your death, Señor. Ogle, take the good Don Diego below and lash him across the mouth of your best cannon. *(He turns to ESTEBAN)* In less than half an hour we shall have your uncle's ship athwart ours, sweeping our decks with her guns. And when they do...Ogle will answer with a full broadside and send them an extra special gift.

ESTEBAN
No, Don Pedro, por favor! In the name of all that's holy!

BLOOD
I fear there is nothing to it, my boy...unless you cooperate exactly as I say. Hagthorpe?

HAGTHORPE
Aye, Captain?

BLOOD
Raise the Spanish ensign.

HAGTHORPE
(Grinning) Aye, Aye, Captain!

(OGLE comes back on board)

BLOOD
Is everything prepared, Ogle?

(A visibly nervous OGLE whispers into BLOOD's ear. BLOOD hesitates before he speaks)

BLOOD
Wolverston, lower a longboat to take Don Esteban and myself across. And load up the chest of gold.

WOLVERSTON
The gold, Cap'n?

BLOOD
It will be a small price to pay if it helps save our ship and our lives, Wolverston.

WOLVERSTON
Aye, aye, Cap'n!

TRANSITION TO SCENE FOURTEEN

WOLVERSTON
As you might recall, Capt'n Blood spoke perfect Castillian Spanish, thanks to his aspendin' two years in that Spanish prison. Thus, he was able to pass perfectly as one of Don Esteban's associates. *(Pronounces the words "RE-call" & "eh-sow-see-ates")*

OGLE
And so the Captain and his captive rowed across to the Encarnacion to meet the Admiral and, perhaps, meet their fate. *(Starts to exit, then turns back)* Oh, we know that most of you don't speak Spanish right well, so we're gonna translate it for you.

Scene Fourteen

(*Lights come up on BLOOD and a nervous ESTEBAN awaiting DON ALÁN*)

BLOOD
And remember, lad, the first shot from the Encarnacion's guns is Ogle's cue to fire the guns of the Cinco Llagas. All of them. I make myself clear, I hope?

ESTEBAN
Si, Don Pedro. Perfectly.

(*DON ALÁN enters and hugs his nephew and kisses him on both cheeks*)

ALÁN
Sobrino! What a joy it is to see you! But why are you here without your father? And who is this you have brought in his stead?

BLOOD
Allow me to introduce to myself. I am Don Pedro Sangre, an unfortunate gentleman of Leon, lately delivered from captivity thanks to the enterprises of your brother.

ALÁN
You are welcome aboard my ship, Don Pedro. But I ask
again, where is my brother and why has he not come
himself, to greet me?

ESTEBAN
Perdone, mi tío, but there is a fever on board and he
could not risk endangering your ship.

ALÁN
A fever! ¡Dios mío! Then why are you two here?

BLOOD
The fever is at its end, Don Alán, and has almost run
its course. Don Esteban was amongst the first to be
infected, but has recovered fully and is not contagious.
I am a physician myself, and had this fever many years
ago, so I was able to minister to the others. We only had
a few men succumb completely to the fever, and we
buried them at sea. Still, we thought it best not to risk
the contagion.

(DON ALÁN makes the sign of the cross)

ALÁN
Muchas gracias, Don Pedro. And may God have mercy
on those poor men's souls. But what is in that chest you
brought over with you?

BLOOD
Twenty-five thousand pieces of eight, which we are to
deliver to your excellency.

ESTEBAN
They are the ransom extracted by my father from the
Governor...

ALÁN
Not another word, in the name of Heaven! I can have

no knowledge of these things! I represent His Catholic
Majesty, who is at peace with the English King. Already
you have said more than it is good for me to know.

ESTEBAN
Then should I return the...items to our own ship,
Uncle?

ALÁN
No, no. You can leave it here. It is...a family matter.
If my brother wishes me to carry some personal items
home to Spain, who am I to tell him no? As long as I
know nothing about it, all is well.

BLOOD
I see that you understand the full nature of your brother's...fever, Don Alán.

ALÁN
Virgen santisima! That brother of mine thinks of everything. Left to myself, I might have committed a fine
indiscretion by venturing aboard his ship. I might have
seen things which, as an Admiral of Spain, it would be
difficult for me to ignore. Now come, let us toast to the
glory of the Spain.

BLOOD
And toast to the damnation of King James, may he rot
on his throne.

ALÁN
Sir, sir, you need my brother here to curb your impudence. The King of England is good friends with His
Catholic Majesty. But since it has been proposed in
private, we will honor it...unofficially.

(DON ALÁN laughs and they all drink)

ESTEBAN
I am afraid, Uncle, that we must depart. My father is in
haste to reach Santo Domingo. He desired me to stay no
longer than necessary to embrace you and...pass along
his belongings.

ALÁN
You are learning well, Esteban. Farewell to you both.
And I hope we meet again, Don Pedro.

BLOOD
I look forward to that day, Don Alán.

TRANSITION TO SCENE FIFTEEN

WOLVERSTON
And as the Cap'n and the young squid rowed back to the Cinco Llagas, we kept a close eye on them.

OGLE
And our cannons trained on the Encarnacion.

SCENE FIFTEEN

(BLOOD, ESTEBAN, PITT, WOLVERSTON, HAGTHORPE, and OGLE are all on deck)

ESTEBAN
And now sirs, when will you release me and my father?

(BLOOD hesitates to answer)

OGLE
I see you haven't told him yet.

ESTEBAN
Have you broken faith, you cur? Has he come to harm?

OGLE
We do not break faith. Don Diego died in his bonds before you ever left this ship.

ESTEBAN
Died? Of what did he die? You killed him, you mean!

OGLE
As I told the captain before you left, when we tied your

father to the cannon, he gave out with a roar of terror
and then collapsed, dead. If I am a judge, Don Diego
died of fear.

*(ESTEBAN strikes OGLE and BLOOD steps between
them)*

ESTEBAN
And you knew this?

BLOOD
Yes.

ESTEBAN
And you did not tell me?

BLOOD
If you had known that...

ESTEBAN
Then you would be hanging from the yardarm of the
Encarnacion at this moment. Well, sir, that fate may still
be yours when my uncle learns the truth.

BLOOD
Take him below. *(One of the men does)* We'll set him
ashore as soon as we are able.

WOLVERSTON
You'll be rememberin' that boy's threats to you, Cap'n.

BLOOD
I care nothing for his threats.

WOLVERSTON
It'd be well if ya did. The wise thing'd be to hang him.

BLOOD
It is not human to be wise. It is much more human to
err.

WOLVERSTON
Aye, Cap'n. It's just out of the ordin'ry to err on the side of mercy.

BLOOD
Then let us always be men who are "out of the ordin'ry", Old Wolf. I've no stomach for cold-blooded killing. At daybreak, pack him into a boat with a keg of water and a sack of hard tack and let him go. Meanwhile, Hagthorp, see if you can find some paint on board this ship. I think it's time to change the name of the Cinco Llagas.

HAGTHORPE
To what, Captain?

BLOOD
The Arabella.

PITT
What's our new course, sir?

BLOOD
We're too short of food and water to try and make Curacao, so we'll change course and sail north to Tortuga.

WOLVERSTON
I reckon ya know that's the haven of pirates, Cap'n.

BLOOD
Precisely, my good Wolverston, precisely. And I think we should fit in there perfectly. Mr. Pitt? Take us out to sea.
PITT
Aye, aye Captain. "But ships shall come from the coast of Kittim, And they shall afflict Asshur and will afflict Eber." *(He pauses as BLOOD crosses away)* "So they also will come to destruction." Numbers 24.

(Music begins)

SONG OF THE LONELY SEA

We once were slaves but now we're free
Heave-ho, heave-ho,
And so it's pirates we will be.
Heave-ho and away we'll go, we're sailing all alone-o.

It's all of us against the world
Heave-ho, heave-ho,
With guns ablaze and flags unfurled
Heave-ho and away we'll go, we're sailing all alone-o.

If we be caught we know we'll hang
Heave-ho, heave-ho,
Or all be shot with a bloody bang.
Heave-ho and away we'll go, we're sailing all alone-o.

They'll sink our ships from 'neath our feet
Heave-ho, heave-ho,
And Davy Jones we'll get to meet.
Heave-ho and away we'll go, we're sailing all alone-o.

The sea she is a mistress cruel
Heave-ho, heave-ho,
To sail her you must be a fool.
Heave-ho and away we'll go, we're sailing all alone-o.
Heave-ho and away we'll go, we're sailing all alone-o.

(The men sing but at some point we see ARABELLA alone staring off to sea on one corner and BLOOD doing the same on the other)

END OF ACT I

(Projections of clouds/sea throughout intermission)

ACT II

REPRISE OF "Song of the Lonely Sea"

In harbor we can sport and play
Heave-ho, heave-ho,
Drink all night and sleep all day.
Heave-ho and away we'll go, we're sailing all alone-o.

But gold is only found at sea
Heave-ho, heave-ho,
So it's a pirate's life for me.
Heave-ho and away we'll go, we're sailing all alone-o.
Heave-ho and away we'll go, we're sailing all alone-o.

OPENING TRANSITION TO SCENE SIXTEEN

HAGTHORPE
So we were forced into the pirate life.

WOLVERSTON
Not as it took much forcin' for some of us.

HAGTHORPE
But Peter could never rid his mind of Arabella Bishop, even though she was beyond his reach forever.

OGLE
And while he may have had the occasional itch to sail to France or Holland, he had no clear goal when he reached there. He was, when all is said, an escaped slave.

WOLVERSTON
An outlaw in his own land.

HAGTHORPE
And a homeless outcast in any other.

OGLE
There remained only the sea, which is free to all, and particularly alluring to those who feel themselves at war with humanity.

SCENE SIXTEEN

(Lights come up on BLOOD and his full crew)

BLOOD

We, the undersigned, are men without a country.
Desperate men, we go to seek a desperate fortune.
Therefore, we do, here and now, band ourselves into
a brotherhood of buccaneers... to practice the trade
of piracy on the high seas. We, the hunted, will now
hunt! Therefore, to that end, we enter into the following Articles of Agreement: We pledge ourselves to be
bound together as brothers in a life and death friendship,
sharing alike in fortune and in trouble. All monies and
valuables which may come into our possession shall be
lumped together into a common fund. If a man conceal
any captured treasure or fail to place it in the general
fund, he shall be marooned. Set ashore on a deserted isle,
and there left with a bottle of water, a loaf of bread and
a pistol with one load. If a man shall be drunk on duty,
he shall receive the same fate. And if a man shall molest a
woman captive... he, too, shall receive the same punishment. These Articles entered into this 20th day of June,

in the year 1687. *(Having finished dictating, he addresses the crew)* Now, men, you've heard the Agreement. It's the world against us and us against the world!

(The men all cheer!)

PITT
"His hand will be against every man, and every man's hand against him." Genesis, 16th chapter, 12th verse.

BLOOD
Those of you in favor of these Articles raise your right hands and say, "Aye!"

(The men all cheer AYE!)

TRANSITION TO SCENE SEVENTEEN

OGLE
And with that began their adventures.

(Images on the Video Screen as they describe the action)

HAGTHORPE
There was a fight in the Windward Passage at the outset with a Spanish Galleon, which ended in the gutting of the Spaniard...

WOLVERSTON
and of his ship as well.

OGLE
There was a daring raid effected by means of several "borrowed" piraguas upon a Spanish pearl fleet in the Rio de la Hacha.

WOLVERSTON
Myself, I were rather fond o'that overland expedition to the goldfields of Santa Maria, on the Spanish Main.

OGLE
And there were lesser adventures, through all of which the crew of the Arabella came with great credit...and even greater profit.

WOLVERSTON
And don't ya know as we all came through, if not unscathed, then at least unbeaten and unbowed.

HAGTHORPE
But in all of our adventures, surprisingly not a single English ship or colony was attacked.

OGLE
So that while the fame of the Arabella and her Captain had swept from the Bahamas to the Windward Isles, from New Providence to Trinidad...

WOLVERSTON
An echo of it had also reached Europe, where the Pirate called Blood was the topic of conversation even at the illustrious court of St. James.

HAGTHORPE
(Clarifying) That's England!

OGLE
And when a problem is discussed at court, a solution is ordered.

HAGTHORPE
A solution as took the form of...

OGLE
(Interrupting him with a "bup, bup, bup") Show, don't tell, my friend. Show, don't tell. All will become clear in time, starting with a meeting on the deck of the HMS Virago, which sailed out of Portsmouth and is now making passage through the Windward Islands, bound for Jamaica.

Scene Seventeen

(*We discover ARABELLA on the deck of a ship. LORD JULIAN approaches*)

JULIAN
Excuse me, my dear, I hope you will forgive my boldness, but as we are going to be traveling together on board this lovely ship, I thought we should become acquainted. My name is Lord Julian Willoughby.

ARABELLA
It's a pleasure to meet you, Lord Julian. I am Arabella Bishop. And please don't think yourself forward. You'll discover that we are much less formal here in the islands.

JULIAN
So I have discovered, and I must say it is a rare treat. Trading the stuffiness of London for the warmth of the West Indies is, I must say, a fair trade.

ARABELLA
So you, too, are sailing for Jamaica? Might I inquire as to what you were doing in Barbardos?

JULIAN
Just a bit of research, shall we say. I am on my way to Jamaica to speak to the newly appointed Governor there, regarding some business of the crown.

ARABELLA
Governor Bishop? Why, he's my uncle! I've just been checking on our plantation and am on my way back to join him.

JULIAN
What a wonderful coincidence! I'm sure your lovely company will make the trip all the more delightful. I find sailing can be so dull.

ARABELLA
Here in the West Indies, we pray for a dull voyage. Lately, the other kind usually involve escaping from pirates.

JULIAN
You mean like that vicious Captain Blood fellow I've heard about.

ARABELLA
(Blushing) No, I was actually referring more to the Spanish pirate, Alán de Panadero. Captain Blood may be a thief and a renegade, but he does not seem to be plying these waters. No, we have more to fear from the Spanish renegades than the English ones.

JULIAN
Really? You seem to have some special insights into the man. I've heard that he was a slave on your island of Barbados. You didn't happen to know him then, did you?

ARABELLA
Actually, yes. (Hesitates) He was a slave on our own plantation.

JULIAN
You don't say! And what manner of man did you find him to be?

ARABELLA
I'd...rather not say. Why do you ask?

JULIAN
I just wish to understand the man better. Why, for instance, does he not attack English ships? He has every legitimate reason to hate the Crown, after all.

ARABELLA
Doesn't every criminal?

JULIAN
Yes and no. They all hate the Crown for convicting them of their crimes. But while I would call that understandable, I would not call it legitimate. They were, after all, guilty of their offenses and should reasonably expect no less than the punishment they earned.

ARABELLA
Precisely. So how does that make Blood different?

JULIAN
Because he really has been treated abominably by the crown.

ARABELLA
He was arrested with a number of other rebels after that skirmish near Bridgewater. I know that for a fact.

JULIAN
Precisely. He was with them but was not of them. He had been called to provide medical attention. When the troops caught up with the rebels, Blood was simply attending to their wounds. He tried to explain it all to the judge, but, well...

ARABELLA
Faith, he's had his revenge now. And that is the thing which has destroyed him.

JULIAN
Revenge? I'm not so sure about that. English pounds are just as tempting to most pirates as Spanish dubloons. I'm of the mind that there may be a reason he has not preyed on English ships to date.

ARABELLA
So he preys solely on the Spanish, Portuguese, Dutch, and French?

JULIAN
Oh no, not the French either. Although there's a clear reason for that.

ARABELLA
Which is?

JULIAN
Tortuga, don't you know.

ARABELLA
I beg your pardon?

JULIAN
The island of Tortuga, where he and his like make their home when their ships need to be refitted or their stores replenished. It's nominally a French port, and the governor there, a Monsiuer d'Ogeron, is very happy to collect some extravagant port fees from the buccaneers and the French are happy to look the other way just so long as the pirates leave French ships alone. Of course, Blood has another reason, or so I was told in Barbados.

ARABELLA
Another reason?

JULIAN
Yes. According to a man I was talking to in the inn last night, it seems that Blood is engaged to M. d'Ogeron's daughter.

ARABELLA
Never!

JULIAN
Well, this fellow seemed to be fairly well-versed in the story. Claims to have lived in Tortuga himself, and from the look of him I could fair believe it. According to him, Blood won the girl from another pirate, some man named Levasseur.

ARABELLA
Won her? What, in a dice game?

JULIAN
(Looking a bit uncomfortable) Not precisely. According to this fellow, and I'm simply repeating what I have been told, mind you, Blood won her...in a sword fight.

ARABELLA
He killed a man for her?

JULIAN
It is an unsavory tale, I'll admit. But men live by different codes out here, it appears.

ARABELLA
And why did this man tell you such a tale? Did he hate this Captain Blood?

JULIAN
I did not gather that. He related it more as, well, just a commonplace.

ARABELLA
A commonplace! How savage.

JULIAN
I dare say that we are all savages under the cloak that civilization fashions for us.

(Their conversation is interrupted by the sound of a horn and men shouting. A SAILOR rushes in)

SAILOR
Beg pardon, your lordship, Miss Bishop, but the captain has ordered you below.

JULIAN
What is happening?

SAILOR
A pair of Spanish ships have been sighted, coming up on us fast. They've got us outgunned. The captain is going to try and outrun them.

ARABELLA
And if he can't?

SAILOR
I'm afraid we'll be at their mercy, my lady.

(Lights fade to the sound of men being commanded to lay on more sail, etc. Various voices are there with lots of screams and yelling, but the voices should NOT include BLOOD, HAGTHORPE, WOLVERSTON, or OGLE. Finally the battle sounds fade as we transition lights up on the narrators)

POSSIBLE LINES TO BE RECORDED FOR BATTLE (final choices left to sound designer and director, but please limit yourselves to these choices):

IN ENGLISH
Shorten those sails!
Gunners, reload your cannons. Faster, men! They're almost on us!
Prepare for borders.
Musketeers, take aim. Make every shot count!
Fire!
Here they come.
Look out, up in the mizzen shrouds!
They've shot away the spritsail yard!
They're coming over the gangway.
There's more coming over the pooprail!

SPANISH ATTACKERS
¡Ataque, hombres!
Subir a bordo, idiotas!
Muerte a los ingleses
¡dispara!
Ahora, ahora, ¡consíguelos!
Fuera de mi camino, pendejos
Mierda!

(And throughout much general noise of black powder weapons, cannons, clashing of swords, screaming of dying men)

TRANSITION TO SCENE EIGHTEEN

OGLE
Alas, as skillful as the English captain was, he was no match for the Spanish ships.

WOLVERSTON
You see, coming up on them from SSW as they was, with the wind from their stern, the English captain's ship was going to have the wind stolen...

(OGLE clears his throat)

WOLVERSTON
I'm starting to sound like Hagthorpe, ain't I?

(OGLE nods)

OGLE
The point is, the captain didn't have a chance. He had no choice but to turn and fight.

WOLVERSTON
Alas, the fight was short-lived. A Spanish broadside holed their ship and the day was won by the Spanish and before you know it, Miss Arabella and her new friend find themselves aboard the Encarnacion, prisoners of Blood's mortal enemy, Don Alán de Panadero.

Scene Eighteen

(Lights come back up on the deck of Don Alán's ship, where we see DON ALÁN and two of his men entering to find ARABELLA and LORD JULIAN)

JULIAN
You dammed Spaniard! What do you mean forcing us on board your ship? I demand you release us. I'm a representative of the His Majesty the King of England.

ALÁN
Don't be a fool, sir, or you and the lady will both come to a fool's end. Besides, even if we did not insist that you stay and enjoy our hospitality, where would you go? Your ship was already sinking. That foolish puppy dog who captained your ship should have surrendered when he had the chance.

JULIAN
What do you intend to do with the rest of the crew?

ALÁN
I have no room for them on board my ships, so we

will leave them adrift in their own longboats. If they survive...? *(Shrugs)* You, two, however... If you please to stay with me?

ARABELLA
Lord Julian, we appear to be out of options.

ALÁN
Allow me to introduce myself. I am Don Alán de Panadero, Admiral of the Navies of his Catholic Majesty Carlos the Second.

JULIAN
Admiral, eh? Then will you tell me why you behave like a damned pirate? You will be made to answer for this day's work and for your violence to this lady and myself.

ALÁN
I offer you no violence. On the contrary, I have save' your lives from a foolish decision made by the puppy dog who captain' your ship.

JULIAN
And what of the lives you have destroyed in wanton butchery? By God, man, they shall cost you dear.

ALÁN
It is possible. All things are possible. Meantime, it is your own lives that will cost you dear. Colonel Bishop is a rich man and will no doubt pay well to have his niece returned. You, my lord, you are rich also, no?

JULIAN
So you are just a damned murderous pirate after all. And you have the impudence to call yourself the Admiral of the Navies of the Catholic King? We shall see what your Catholic King will have to say about this.

ALÁN

I have treat' you English heretic dogs just as you have treat' Spaniards upon the seas. You robbers and thieves out of hell! I have the honesty to do it in my own name, but you, you perfidious beasts! You send your Captain Bloods and your Morgans against us and deny responsibility for what they do. Like Pilate, you wash your hands. Well, let Spain play the part of Pilate for a change. Let Spain deny responsibility for me, when your ambassador at the Escurial shall go whining and mewling to the Supreme Council.

JULIAN

(Calmly) I will tell you what I told the Spanish Ambassador. Blood is not an admiral of England.

ALÁN

Is he not? How do I know? How does Spain know? Are you not liars all, you English?

JULIAN

I never lie, sir. I am a diplomat.

ARABELLA

And it sorts with all I have heard of you and your honor that you have chosen to insult a man who is unarmed and your prisoner.

(The insult to his honor is more than he can bear, so DON ALÁN storms out with his men following)

JULIAN

That wasn't very nice, Miss Bishop.

ARABELLA

I'm sorry, but the insult was well deserved.

JULIAN

Oh, most certainly. I was simply complaining that you

beat me to it.

ARABELLA
I don't understand how all this can happen. At Bridgetown three years ago there was a Spanish raid, and things were done that should have been impossible to men. Horrible things which strain belief. And they claim to be men who follow God! Are men just beasts?

JULIAN
Not all men. But some men, yes. And as for following God? Well, the church is an institution made up of men, made up by men. And as such, it suffers from the same diseases men have. Bigotry. Hatred.

ARABELLA
Maybe we should try an institution made up by women, for a change.

JULIAN
It might be worth a try. You certainly could not do any worse, I think.

TRANSITION TO SCENE NINETEEN

OGLE
And so Don Alán's ship sailed on, steering a north by
westerly course, heading up towards the Greater Antilles,
then veering to the southwest round Cape Tiburon on
the coast of Haiti.

HAGTHORPE
How comes when I do it, I'm told it's too much, but
when Ogle does it, it's okay?

WOLVERSTON
Panache, Hagthorpe. Panache. *(Pronounces the second
syllable to rhyme with "cash")*

OGLE
Until, standing well out to sea, with the land no more
than a cloudy outline to larboard

HAGTHORPE
That's the same as starboard. Means to the right. *(He is
shushed)*

OGLE
She ran straight into the arms of Captain Blood, who
was marking for the Windward Passage on his way back
to Tortuga.

WOLVERSTON
Ironic, ain't it? Now some folks will scoff at such things as coincidence.

OGLE
But open the history of the past to whatsoever page you will, and there you shall find coincidence at work, bringing about events that the merest chance might have averted.

HAGTHORPE
(Putting on a very learned air) A wise man one said that "Coincidence may be defined as the very tool used by Fate to shape the destinies of men and nations."

WOLVERSTON
That's fine. Who said that?

HAGTHORPE
Some guy named Rafael Sabatini.

WOLVERSTON
Now, ya know the Cap'n could've avoided this battle, seeing as he be outnumbered two to one. But something inside him drove him to accept the Spaniard's challenge, 'though he be outnumbered and outgunned.

OGLE
And on board the Encarnacion, Lord Julian and Arabella could only watch and pray.

SCENE NINETEEN

(The three ships are defined by the three areas of the set design: Blood's ship is Center and two Spanish ships indicated by projections SL and SR. ARABELLA and JULIAN are either SL or SR as they are on one of the ships as they narrate the battle. The action they are describing is created by the lights and sounds the actions of the men on board Blood's ship)

(BATTLE DIALOGUE)

ALÁN
Patience, men! Hold your fire until we have him. He's sailing straight to his doom.

JULIAN
Miss Arabella, time to take cover.

ARABELLA
Not on your life, Lord Julian. I can see best from here. If this is my end, I want to see it coming.

JULIAN

That captain must be mad! He's driving straight into a death-trap. The Spanish guns will blow his ships to splinters from both sides at once.

(Trumpets blare and guns are fired. We hear the sounds of cannons striking a ship and wood rending and men screaming. When the cannon balls are fired, the men on the ship must recoil and when they hit another ship, the actors on that one must be jolted by the impact)

ARABELLA

The Englishman has drawn first blood! They took out the entire bowsprit! We're yawing to port.

JULIAN

Any closer, and it's going to be our blood he's drawing. Wait. The Spanish guns have stopped firing. I don't understand.

ARABELLA

Don't you see? The Englishman has outmaneuvered them! By sailing between them, he's pulled their teeth. If they fire at him, they risk missing and...

JULIAN

And hitting their own sister ship! Damme, but that was a brave chance that captain took.

ARABELLA

And now they're unloading both broadsides at the Spanish ships!

(Sound of thirty-six cannons being fired almost simultaneously. This could be the loudest sound in the entire show)

JULIAN

Look, the pirates have holed the other ship below the

waterline. It's going down by its head. But what's that pirate captain doing now?

ARABELLA
He's coming around again. He must be mad. I think he means to ram us.

JULIAN
Look out!

BLOOD
Stations! *(Crew member relays the order)*

(Sounds of two ships coming together hard, which throws JULIAN and ARABELLA off balance)

JULIAN
What's Don Alán doing?

ARABELLA
This ship has been holed. He's leading his men aboard the pirate ship!

(Sights and sounds of men boarding Blood's ship. Spanish blasphemies and English curses are heard, or not, depending on sound design and direction)

ENGLISH
You scullion! You rampallian! You fustilarian! I'll tickle your catastrophe!
Go, prick your face, you lily-liver'd boy.
C'mon you clay-brained knotty-pated fool, you whoreson obscene greasy tallow-catch!
You eel-skin, you dried neat's-tongue, you bull's-pizzle, you stock-fish
Take that, you pox ridden son of a whore! You're unfit for any place but hell."
Come get it, you pigeon-livered loons
Have at ya, ya puke-stocking Spanish pouch!

SPANISH
El burro sabe mas que tu
Eres tan feo/a que hiciste llorar a una cebolla
Me cago en tu puta madre
Que te folle un pez
Ven a probar mi espada

(We see men running back and forth and chasing and killing, culminating with BLOOD and DON ALÁN find each other. While all of this has been happening, we should see JULIAN and ARABELLA making their way across to Blood's ship, with ARABELLA taking the lead and Julian being forced to follow. Lines/orders that BLOOD gives can include the following, as appropriate to the final staging. More lines can be added as the scene is blocked)

BLOOD
Look out up in the futtock shrouds, men! As soon as they clear that rail, fire your pistols! Alright, my hearties, stay with me.

(Finally BLOOD and ALÁN confront each other)

BLOOD
We meet again, Don Alán, although not, perhaps as you might wish. *(BLOOD gives him an elegant bow)* You are welcome to surrender now.

(DON ALÁN attacks)

BLOOD
You are a brave man. Braver, it seems, than your brother.

ALÁN
Now you give me double reason to avenge his death, Perro Ingles!

(They fight)

ALÁN
You should give up your love of the English, Capitan,
and join us. There is much is Spain you could profit by.

BLOOD
We're doing our best to profit from you Spanish already.
One ship at a time.

*(They continue the fight and we see a Spanish sailor
sneaking up behind BLOOD. ARABELLA spots him
picks up a fallen sword or cutlass, and engages him, killing him)*

BLOOD
You seem to be making a habit of saving my life, Miss
Bishop.

ARABELLA
You seem to be making a habit of needing it. Who saves
you when there's no woman around, I wonder?

BLOOD
Tell me, whatever happened to young Esteban?

ALÁN
He returned to Spain, where he will live out his life in
shame.

BLOOD
At least he will live out his life, my friend.

*(In the end, BLOOD has disarmed DON ALÁN without
killing him)*

ALÁN
What do you intend by me?

BLOOD
(Shrugs and smiles) All that I intend has already been
accomplished. And lest it increase your rancor, I beg you

to observe that you have brought it all upon yourself. Your longboats are being launched. You are at liberty to embark in them with your men before we scuttle your ship. Yonder are the shores of Hispaniola. You should make them safely. And if you'll take my advice, sir, you'll not hunt me again. I think I am unlucky to you. Get you home to Spain, Don Alán, back to your nephew and to concerns that you understand better than this trade of the sea.

(DON ALÁN exits, a beaten man)

JULIAN
You mean you'll let him go free?

BLOOD
What should I do with him?

JULIAN
Well, he is a pirate.

BLOOD
So am I. I'm not sure who the devil you are, but you and Miss Bishop are welcome aboard my ship, unless you fancy a trip to Hispaniola with Don Alán.

JULIAN
I'm not sure which is the frying pan and which is the fire. Who, exactly, might you be, sir?

ARABELLA
Didn't you know, Lord Julian? This is the man you've been looking for. This is Captain Blood.

JULIAN
So this man is a friend of yours?

ARABELLA
I'm not sure I'd use that word, my lord. I do not account

a thief and pirate as being amongst my friends. Now might I suggest that we follow his advice, just this once.

(ARABELLA puts her arm through LORD JULIAN's and they exit)

BLOOD
Thief and pirate. Thief and pirate.

(He exits)

TRANSITION TO SCENE TWENTY

HAGTHORPE
And now that the Captain and Miss Arabella are both on board the same ship, all will be well, right?

WOLVERSTON
He don't know much about women, do he?

OGLE
About as much as he knows about ships, my friend.

WOLVERSTON
The Cap'n manages to avoid Miss Arabella for a day or so, but there is only so much room to hide on board a ship, even for a man as clever as the Cap'n.

Scene Twenty

(BLOOD and JULIAN meet on deck)

BLOOD
It appears that you suffered some good fortune as a result of Don Alán finally locating me, Lord Julian.

JULIAN
It is fortuitous in more ways than one, sir. For you are the very man I've come to the Indies hoping to find.

BLOOD
And why, pray tell, would you be looking for me? I am, as it's been pointed out, a thief and a pirate. Is there a price on my head, now?

JULIAN
You misapprehend me completely, sir. I am here on behalf of the Crown to make you an offer.

BLOOD
And what kind of an offer would that be?

JULIAN
Might I ask you a question, first?

BLOOD
You're a curious one, but have at it.

JULIAN
Why have you chosen not to attack English ships?

BLOOD
(Pauses before answering) English ships are poor. Leave it to the English to come to a place like the New World and settle everywhere there's no gold and no spices worth trading. If it weren't for sugar and rum, the English would have nothing. And those cargoes aren't worth stealing.

JULIAN
Excuse my skepticism, Captain, but I'm not sure that's entirely the answer. However, we shall let it stand. The simple truth is that because you've made that choice, for whatever reason, I've been sent to make you an offer. The same one we made to the pirate Morgan some twenty years ago. I've brought with me a Letter of Marque signed by the King. We'd like to offer you a commission in the King's Navy. You could go right ahead attacking Spanish ships, but now you'd have a legal reason to do so.

BLOOD
I thought that England wasn't at war with Spain.

JULIAN
Ah, well, let us say that this is a situation we believe is about to change. So will you accept the King's commission?

BLOOD
You are my guest aboard this ship, and I still have some

notion of decent behavior left me, thief and pirate though I may be. So I'll not tell you what I think of you for daring to bring me the King's offer.

(BLOOD crosses away and we here JULIAN muttering to himself)

JULIAN
Thief and pirate. Oh, my.

(PITT, HAGTHORPE, WOLVERSTON enter as JULIAN exits)

PITT
What are your orders, Captain?

BLOOD
Make speed to Port Royale, Jamaica, Jeremy. We need to drop off Lord Julian and Miss Bishop there. Wolverston, put on every bit of canvas those yards can hold.

(BLOOD begins to exit. The crewman stand there stunned at what has just happened. BLOOD turns back. LORD JULIAN cannot hear the next lines)

BLOOD
What are you men still doing here? We've got to get Miss Bishop and her fiancé back where they belong.

(BLOOD exits)

WOLVERSTON
Fiancé? That means they're getting married, don't it?

HAGTHORPE
It does indeed, Wolf, my friend.

WOLVERSTON
Well, at least we know what's been a'sticking in the cap'n's gullet.

HAGTHORPE
So what do we do?

WOLVERSTON
Same as always, my friend. Follow orders.

HAGTHORPE
Aye. Make speed to Port Royale. There's a gallows waiting there for every one of us, but I guess no man should
be late to his own hanging.

(They exit and ARABELLA enters)

BLOOD
Ah, there you are Miss Bishop. I was hoping to see you.
It is odd how a person can know himself and what he
truly is, and yet later be shocked to find that others
agree with him. Thank you for providing that lesson,
Miss Bishop.

(BLOOD exits)

JULIAN
He amazes me, Madam. That he should alter his course
for us is amazing in itself. What is even more amazing
is that he has done so after the way you spoke to him.

ARABELLA
I beg your pardon?

JULIAN
Calling him a thief and pirate?

ARABELLA
I usually call things by their names.

JULIAN
Do you? Stab me! I shouldn't boast of it. It argues either
extreme youth or extreme foolishness. As does a display
of ingratitude.

ARABELLA
So only the young are ungrateful?

JULIAN
(Feeling a bit peevish himself) I did not say so, madam. For if unlike you I do not always say precisely what I think, I do say precisely what I mean. To be ungrateful is human. To display it purposefully is childish. Especially to man like Blood. Damme me if I ever met a man I liked better, or even a man I liked as well. Yet there's nothing to be done. I wonder, now, if the mischief is of your working. Your words have rankled with him. He threw them at me again and again. He refused to take the King's commission.

ARABELLA
Commission?

JULIAN
Oh, yes. I offered him the King's own Letter of Marque. Would have made him an admiral. He turned it down. What's to be done with a fellow like that? He'll end up swinging from a yardarm for all his luck. And the quixotic fool is running into danger at the present moment on our behalf.

ARABELLA
How?

JULIAN
How? Haven't you heard? He's sailing to Jamaica, the headquarters of the English Fleet.

ARABELLA
But there is no hope for him in that! He has no more bitter enemy in the world than my uncle.

JULIAN
Well, perhaps there is yet a way to change both of them a bit.

ARABELLA
My uncle will never give in.

JULIAN
He may not have a choice, my dear.

(BLOOD enters)

BLOOD
I need to talk with you, Lord Julian.

ARABELLA
And do you always interrupt conversations without so much as an apology, Captain?

BLOOD
Miss Bishop, did your uncle give you my present?

ARABELLA
What present?

BLOOD
The ten pounds I gave him, with which I brought myself back from you.

(She looks uncomfortable)

ARABELLA
Yes, he did.

BLOOD
Then please remember I am no longer your slave. I am the Captain of this ship. Perhaps you should return to your cabin, Miss Bishop. You would certainly find it preferable to being in the company of...

ARABELLA
...a thief and pirate? Perhaps I would. Besides, what would your fiancé think of your standing on the deck alone with another woman?

BLOOD
Fiancé? *(He laughs)* And who would marry a man such as I?

ARABELLA
(Confused) I had heard that you were engaged to the daughter of M. d'Ogeron.

BLOOD
(Smiling) Ah, I see. And what else have your heard about my...impending marriage.

ARABELLA
I've heard how you won her by the murder of another man who had claim to her.

BLOOD
(Visibly upset) Murder!

ARABELLA
Yes, murder. Did you not murder another pirate named Levasseur?

BLOOD
(Chuckling wryly) So someone told you about that?

ARABELLA
Do you deny it?

BLOOD
I killed him, it is true. Just as I killed another man in similar circumstances. That was in Bridgetown on the night of the Spanish Raid. You were there. As was Mary Trail.

JULIAN
Well, well, well. There may be more to this thief and pirate than some folks believe. You've a past score to wipe out, man! You've done something towards it, I confess, and you've shown your quality in doing so. And that's why I'm urging you once more to accept the commission from the King.

BLOOD
Your lordship is very good, but...

ARABELLA
Peter, there is no "but" to it! If you want your past forgotten and your future opened up, this is your chance. Your duty lies here.

BLOOD
My duty to the King?

JULIAN
Not to the King, but England. The country is all, sir; the sovereign naught. Kings come and pass; England remains, to be honorably served by her sons, whatever rancor they may hold against the man who rules her in their time.

BLOOD
Do you suppose now that this honorable service might redeem one who was a thief and pirate?

ARABELLA
If he...needs redeeming. Perhaps...perhaps he has been judged too harshly.

BLOOD
Why, if you think that, life might have its uses after all. But I could never serve King James.

JULIAN
King James? I'm not the representative of James, I'm the representative of King William.

BLOOD
King William? And who may be King William, and of what may he be king when he's at home?

ARABELLA
Oh my. He hasn't heard! He's talking about William of Orange.

JULIAN
I beg your pardon, madam. Please refer to our sovereign as His Majesty King William III. Who, with Queen Mary, has now been ruling England for five months and more.

BLOOD
Do you mean, sir, that they've roused themselves at home and kicked out that pimple James and his pack of hounds?

JULIAN
His politics are very sound, I see.

ARABELLA
Indeed, my lord.

JULIAN
The English people will only go so far, Captain Blood, and then they get up on their stubborn hind legs. It simply took some of us longer to get there than you.

BLOOD
Well, if it's this King William I'm to serve, then maybe I'll rethink that commission, my lord. I'll have to take some time, though, to adjust my view of the world.

(Voice from above or offstage, in the crow's nest)

HARPER
Ahoy, below! Ship's wreckage off the port bow *(Can be starboard, if that works for show's blocking)*. And there looks to be someone floating in the water.

BLOOD
Hold her steady, Jeremy.

(MIDSHIPMAN MALLARD is pulled aboard. The man sits on the edge of the Poopdeck)

BLOOD
Take it easy, man, you're safe now.

JULIAN
What happened, my good man?

MALLARD
I was on the HMS Standard, a frigate out of Portsmouth. We had just left Port Royale when we were surprised by them, my lord. A lucky shot set off our magazine and blew up the entire ship. I was blown clear and managed to grab ahold of one of the yardarms that was floating. I've been out there for hours and had about given up hope when you came along.

ARABELLA
You mean to tell us there's another Spanish ship out there?

MALLARD
No, ma'am.

JULIAN
Then who was it?

MALLARD
It was the French, my lord.

BLOOD
But we're not at war with the French.

JULIAN
I fear that we must be, Peter. I knew there was trouble brewing when I left, but damme me if they haven't jumped the gun. That blasted Louis must have sent word to his navy to try and catch us by surprise.

ARABELLA
And it looks as if he has.

JULIAN
But why would any French admiral be foolish enough to attack Port Royale. He'd be facing our entire West Indies fleet.

MALLARD
I'm afraid not, my Lord. The fleet has left Port Royale.

BLOOD
What do you mean, man?

MALLARD
They've sailed to Tortuga. Governor Bishop is leading the expedition himself. He swore he'd clean out that nest of pirates once-and-for-all.

(MALLARD is led off)

JULIAN
That rascal Bishop shall answer for this with his head. What would make him desert his post and take the entire fleet with him? Is he mad?

BLOOD
It wasn't madness, it was vindictiveness. It's me he's hunting at Tortuga, my lord. So I guess that it's up to me to be looking after Jamaica for King William!

JULIAN
But we're not equal to it, damme my eyes! You heard the man, the French have three ships bearing down on the port. And any one of them is a match for yours.

ARABELLA
In guns—aye! But it should be clear to even you, by now, that there's more than guns to these affairs.

BLOOD
You heard the lady, my lord. It seems you're about to see just a bit more action.

(We hear the sound of distant cannons. Lookout calls from above)

HARPER
Captain! Port Royale dead ahead. And there's a battle going on.

BLOOD
What can you see, Harper?

HARPER
Looks like three French ships, Captain. The fort is firing back at 'em, but two of the ships are almost past it. (Pause) The third seems to be in trouble, though, Captain.

BLOOD
Time to cut our speed. Haul off some of that canvas, men!

JULIAN
But why? The Port is under attack!

BLOOD
I'll not be trying your patience much longer. But it's this way now: there's nothing at all to be gained by haste, and a deal to be gained by delaying.

JULIAN
You think Bishop's fleet will show up if we delay long enough?

ARABELLA
Hardly! What he's hoping for is that the French are as lubberly as usual and get too close to the fort.

BLOOD
Indeed, she's right. With a little luck, the fort may take one of their ships off the board and leave us with just two.

JULIAN
And then you'll play them as you did the Spanish?

BLOOD
I fear, my lord, that card's not in the game this time. Jeremy, stand by your helm and keep her heading two points larboard of the harbor entrance. It looks like you're in for another battle, I fear, Lord Julian.

JULIAN
Dear me, but I'm going to have a great deal to answer for after this.

BLOOD
With the King?

JULIAN
No. With my wife.

BLOOD
Wife? But I thought...

JULIAN
Thought what, my good sir?

BLOOD
Thought that I was a fool, that's all, Lord Julian. And it appears I am.

(HAGTHORPE has entered)

BLOOD
Do we have an English flag on board, Hagthorpe

HAGTHORPE
We have every manner of flag on board, sir, including a lady's purple petticoat.

BLOOD
Well, hoist the colors and take us in. Wait, I have a better idea. When an English lamb creeps up on a nest of French foxes, he does well to wear a bushy tail. Hoist the French flag, instead. Keep her trimmed by the head, Mister Pitt! If we can get close enough, we can take out the second ship and then the third will retreat, you can count on it.

JULIAN
How do you know?

WOLVERSTON
Because they're French! They ain't got no stomach for a fair fight.

(The following dialogue is accompanied by the appropriate sounds)

BLOOD
Put the helm over, Jeremy! Forward men to your stations. *(Crewman relays "stations!)* Furl the topsails and the mainsails. Strip to the mizzen and the bowsprit. Let loose with the bow chasers, now. Let her know we're here. Ogle, prepare a broadside your musketeers and let's hope your men have gotten their eyes from you.

HAGTHORPE
Peter, they've shot away the mizzenmast!

BLOOD
Cut the mizzenstays and the ratlines! Let 'er go!

HAGTHORPE
We've been holed, Peter. She's bilging!

BLOOD
We've got to keep her head up. Jettison the forward guns and anchors. Anything you can! Hard over now, Jeremy, straight into them before they recover their wits. Keep all the sails on, men. (*Crew member relays "Sails on!"*) We're outgunned. Our only hope is to ram her before we sink. Stand by, there! Wolverston, prepare to board!

WOLVERSTON
It's a desperate chance you're taking, Cap'n.

BLOOD
Desperate? It's positively foolhardy, Old Wolf! But remember, "Fortis fortuna adiuvat." Fortune favors the brave, my friend. Ogle, pass the word to the gunner in the prow to fire as fast as he can load. Bring us close now, men! Musketeers to their stations!

OGLE
Peter, we're taking on water below decks.

BLOOD
Arabella, it looks like I'll have to let you board after all. Stay close to me.

ARABELLA
Of course, I will. How else can I protect you? After all, you need to think about your fiancé.

BLOOD
I've told you, I have no fiancé!

ARABELLA
Well, maybe we can do something about that, if we both
survive this battle.

*(BLOOD looks startled, then pulls her into an embrace
and they exchange a very long, passionate kiss. Long
enough to make the audience start to giggle)*

ARABELLA
Now hadn't we better get on with this?

BLOOD
Follow me, men! It's time to board her. Be quick about
it, unless you want to go swimming today!

*(The crew yells "BLOOD!" And then they race into
battle. The rest of this scene is played almost entirely
with sound—we don't see most of the battle, simply
flashes of it, with a moment of two men fighting here
and then a couple of others fighting over there. We never
see BLOOD nor ARABELLA and do not know their
fate. Almost all is pre-recorded, with the sounds of pistol
shots, cannon fire, ships crashing together, bugles, wood
being rended, waves crashing aboard ship, men shouting,
clashing of swords. And for the only time in the play
we might see the smoke from the cannon, obscuring all
upstage. In the end we hear the sound of men cheering)*

(DIALOGUE TO INCLUDE IN THE BATTLE)

WOLVERSTON
C'mon ya sons of biscuit eaters!

BLOOD
Take it to them, boys! And do it handsomely. They've
already been measured for their chains.

WOLVERSTON
That's right, Hagthorpe. Cleave that bilge-sucking scum

right to the brisket.

BLOOD
Ogle, look out! Up on the poop! *(Sound of a gunshot)*

HAGTHORPE
That'll teach 'em to sneak up on my mate.

(French blasphemies and English curses are heard, including the following:)

FRENCH
Mon dieu! On est a l'áttaque!
C'est les Anglais!
Voyons, ils s'embarquent!
Au secours! Au secours!
Je vais te casser la gueule!
Sacre bleu!
Allez au diable!
Putain de merde!
Dégage, cabot Anglais!
Ca me fait chier
Oh putain

ENGLISH
By St. Boogar and all the saints at the backside door of purgatory! To blazes with ya, ya passel of flaming frogs! Great horn spoon! That's one for Captain Blood! Dad-sizzle, I'll rip you from gullet to gate!

(There is a sound of cheering that fades off as we transition)

Scene Twenty-One

(A neutral space that functions as the Governor's office. The scene opens as BISHOP is led in by a WOLVERSTON, now dressed as a guard)

BISHOP
You can't arrest me.

WOLVERSTON
I've got my orders, sir.

BISHOP
Orders? From who?

WOLVERSTON
Orders of the governor, sir.

BISHOP
Governor? You're mad. I am the governor.

(LORD JULIAN enters)

JULIAN
You mean you were the governor.

BISHOP
What? And who are you?

JULIAN
Lord Julian Willoughby, special emissary from his Majesty the King. Bishop, you've been broken for abandoning your post in time of war.

BISHOP
What?

JULIAN
Despite being told of the declaration of war, you went off on some wild goose chase, leaving your city at the mercy of the enemy. It's possible that the charge of treason lies against you.

BISHOP
Treason! You can't charge me with treason.

JULIAN
I fear that decision is out of my hands, "Les carottes sont cuites."

BISHOP
Why does everyone think spouting Latin is clever.

JULIAN
Actually, that was French. "The carrots are cooked." The decision has been made, as it were. By the new governor. It rests entirely with him whether you are hanged or not.

BISHOP
This is all Blood's fault!

(ARABELLA enters)

BISHOP
Arabella! What are you doing here?

ARABELLA
Pleading for you with the governor, Uncle. As the richest landowner in the Caribbean, I hoped he would listen
to me.

BISHOP
You...the richest...what do you mean?

ARABELLA
Haven't you been paying attention to the calendar,
Uncle? I turned twenty-five today. Which means control
and ownership of the plantation reverts to me. But alas,
the governor was not impressed by money. So I told
him that if he would be as merciful as you were cruel, I
would marry him. And he accepted my proposal.

BISHOP
What?

(BLOOD enters the room followed by what appears to be
a guard)

BISHOP
Well, so they've captured you at last. At least I'll have the
pleasure of seeing you hanged.

JULIAN
That will be up to the governor, I think.

(BLOOD comes to center stage and ARABELLA runs to
meet him and kisses him)

BISHOP
Arabella! What do you think you're doing!

ARABELLA
Kissing my husband.

BISHOP
What? But what about the governor?

ARABELLA
Oh, the governor won't mind.

(They kiss again)

BISHOP
How can you say that?

(They finally break the kiss. BLOOD smiles)

BLOOD
Because I'm the new governor. Lord Julian, what new
business have you brought me today?

REPRISE OF THE OPENING SONG

For it's CAPTAIN BLOOD who's the pirate
they all dread.
He'll plunge in pursuit, then plunder your loot
and leave your ship for dead.
And it's BLOOD, BLOOD, BLOOD 'cross the
sea and 'neath the sky.
So it's Captain Blood we'll trust and love and
follow 'til we die.
Here's to BLOOD, BLOOD, BLOOD, yes to
BLOOD, BLOOD, BLOOD,
CAPTAIN BLOOD!

CURTAIN

ABOUT THE PLAYWRIGHT

DAVID RICE is Co-Founder (with his late wife Alison C. Vesely) of First Folio Theatre, where he has produced over 70 productions which have earned 40 Jeff Nominations and 7 Joseph Jefferson Awards for Excellence in Chicago Theater.

As a playwright, David specializes in adaptations. His plays include *SHREW'D!*; *CYMBELINE: A MUSICAL FOLK TALE* (Joseph Jefferson Awards – Original Adaptation and Original Music); *THE MADNESS OF EDGAR ALLAN POE: A LOVE STORY* (Jeff Nomination – Original Adaptation); *THE CASTLE OF OTRANTO*; and Dean Monti's *WHY DOGS DON'T TALK*. Trivia lovers may be interested to know that David was a four-time winner on *Jeopardy!* He is a proud member of both the Dramatists Guild and Actors Equity Association.

ABOUT THE AUTHOR

RAFAEL SABATINI (1875-1950) was an Italian born novelist. Born to an English mother and an Italian father, he was educated in Italy, Portugal, and Switzerland, before moving to Liverpool at the age of 17.

He began his writing career at the age of 20, and by 1899 was selling short works to first class national magazines like *Pearson's Magazine*, *London Magazine*, and *Royal Magazine*. His true fame did not come about, however, until 1920, with the publication of SCARAMOUCHE followed in 1921 by CAPTAIN BLOOD. The success of those works led to a greater interest in one of his earlier novels, THE SEA HAWK.

Sabatini enjoyed his greatest success during the 1930's, a period which saw Hollywood embrace his novels as the perfect vehicles for action star Errol Flynn. The last great film based on a Sabatini novel was the 1952 SCARAMOUCHE featuring Stewart Granger, which was released two years after Sabatini's death.

MORE FROM SORDELET INK

PLAYSCRIPTS

WWW.SORDELETINK.COM

SORDELET INK NOVELS BY DAVID BLIXT

NELLIE BLY
WHAT GIRLS ARE GOOD FOR
CHARITY GIRL
CLEVER GIRL

THE STAR-CROSS'D SERIES
THE MASTER OF VERONA
VOICE OF THE FALCONER
FORTUNE'S FOOL
THE PRINCE'S DOOM
VARNISH'D FACES: STAR-CROSS'D SHORT STORIES

WILL & KIT
HER MAJESTY'S WILL

THE COLOSSUS SERIES
COLOSSUS: STONE & STEEL
COLOSSUS: THE FOUR EMPERORS

EVE OF IDES—A PLAY

NON-FICTION
SHAKESPEARE'S SECRETS: ROMEO & JULIET
TOMORROW, AND TOMORROW: ESSAYS ON MACBETH
FIGHTING WORDS

THE MYSTERY OF CENTRAL PARK

A rejected marriage proposal and the corpse of a dead beauty confound Dick Treadwell's hopes for happiness, until his beloved Penelope sets him a task: she will marry him if he solves— *the Mystery of Central Park!*

EVA, THE ADVENTURESS

Nellie Bly's ripped-from-the-headlines novel of a poor girl determined to revenge herself upon the world, only to find that, in the battle between love and revenge, only one can triumph.

NEW YORK BY NIGHT

Setting out to solve the bold diamond robbery, millionaire detective Lionel Dangerfield finds himself in competition with Ruby Sharpe, daring young reporter for the *New York Planet*. Will "The Danger" solve the case before Ruby can steal the story—and his heart?

ALTA LYNN, M.D.

A prank goes awry and Alta Lynn finds herself wed against her will. Leaving love behind, she throws herself into the study of medicine, only to find that love has other plans for her!

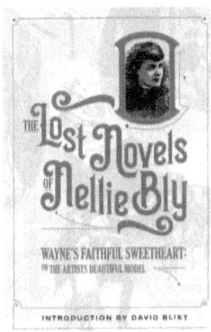

WAYNE'S FAITHFUL SWEETHEART

Beautiful Dorette Lover is rescued from poverty when she finds work as an artist's model. That same day she witnesses a seeming murder. To protect the man accused, she agrees to become his bride—only to fall desperately in love with him!

LITTLE LUCKIE

Luckie Thurlow longs for to be accepted by society and gain the man she loves. But she harbors a dark secret—she is the daughter of the murderous Gypsy Queen, who plans to use Luckie to gain her own revenge!

IN LOVE WITH A STRANGER

Kit Clarendon is in love! Trouble is, she doesn't know her love's name. But she is determined to track him down and force him to love her! A wild pursuit filled with disguises, desperate deeds, and declarations of love as Kit determines to go through fire and water to win him!

THE LOVE OF THREE GIRLS

An heiress in disguise, a factory girl with dreams of wealth, and a sweet child of charity are forced into rivalry when they all fall in love with the same man! Murder, fever, fallen women, and a desperate villain conspire against—
the love of three girls!